TEMPTED

ALSO BY LARAMIE BRISCOE

The Haldonia Monarchy

Royal Rebel

Royal Chaos

Royal Love

A GRIZZLY RIVER RANCH NOVEL

He's the kind of trouble
worth breaking every rule for.

LARAMIE BRISCOE

Tempted

Paperback Edition

Love N. Books Press
An Imprint of Wolfpack Publishing
1707 E. Diana Street
Tampa, FL 33610

www.lovenbookspress.com

Edited by My Brother's Editor
Cover Design by Pilcrow Design

Paperback ISBN 979-8-89567-721-6
Ebook ISBN 979-8-89567-720-9
LCCN

TEMPTED

ONE
AUBREE

THEY SAY you can't go home again. But some of us don't have a choice. Not when our entire lives come crashing down at our feet.

Dust. All over the fucking place.

It's the first thing that hits me as I make my way out of the airport in Grizzly River, South Dakota. Coughing, I put my hand up to shield my eyes from the bright sun, checking the trucks parked in front of the entrance for one person.

My older brother.

"Aubree, get the fuck over here. We gotta go."

There. He. Is. Always in a hurry, and never one to care too much about what his little sister has going on. "Thanks, I got my suitcase and everything."

He raises an eyebrow as he looks over at me. It's affectionate, but it also says let's fucking go. "There's a lot going on at the ranch today, Aubs. We gotta get back."

Hurrying over to where he left his truck idling, I hop in the passenger seat while he puts my suitcase in the back. Within minutes, he's behind the wheel, and we take off with another cloud of dust behind us.

The weather in North Dakota is a crapshoot. Judging by the amount of dust that's hanging around, it hasn't been much of a wet spring. Glancing at the median as we pass by, I see we need some rain.

"Was your flight okay?" Truett asks, seeming to slow down for a moment, allowing himself to stop going a million miles a minute.

I don't actually believe he cares to know. He's always thinking about what else he has to do for the day. It's how he's been since he took custody of me. "It was decent," I shrug. "Wish you would've let me get first class." I shoot him a glare. "It's not like we can't afford it."

"It was two hours, you brat. You didn't need first class for two hours. I have to clean up the shit you left behind anyway," he reminds me.

Right, the entire reason I had to leave Chicago with my tail tucked between my legs. Running home was my first and only option, but it wasn't my favorite. I hate having Truett fix what I broke. "The rest of my stuff will be here next week."

"Yeah." He comes to a stop at the end of Main Street, looks both ways, and then accelerates out into the county, toward our childhood home. "I got a notification when they sent me the bill."

Of course he's going to throw that back in my face. "I'm sorry." I swallow roughly. "About all of this. I know it isn't easy, and I'm the reason..."

He grips the steering wheel tighter. "Look, we can't change

it. We just have to deal with it. When Mom and Dad died, I took custody of you, Aubree. I take that shit seriously."

"I know you do." He always had. From the moment we got the knock on the door, and then I had to go and fuck it up. We may not see eye-to-eye, and he leaves a lot to be desired when it comes to showing me unconditional love, but he's always been there for me. He's the only person I've ever been able to count on. "Thank you. Thank you for letting me come home."

His gaze doesn't waver from where he's staring out at the road in front of us. "You can always come home. Your room will always be your room, even if I have a wife and kids. You're my kid sister. I gave up a lot to keep a roof over our heads, and I'll always do that. I just know you didn't want to come back."

That's the understatement of the year. My life, actually.

"What are your plans? Do you have any?" he asks. His plans have plans. If there's one thing Truett does, it's prepare for what may happen. Every contingency has a contingency.

Other than lick my wounds? "I haven't given it much thought yet. I figured I'd help you around the ranch. Even though I haven't lived on it for seven years, I still do know my way around."

"We can always use the help, but don't feel like you have to do something you don't want to do. You know as well as I do, it's hard work."

"Maybe that's what I need," I sigh, my gaze traveling over the rolling hills. I'd learned to ride a horse on terrain just like this. I think I need that again. "To get my hands dirty, for my muscles to be sore. Do you know I don't have calluses on my fingers anymore?" I hold them up so he can see.

"That's okay, Aubs. I sent you to college so that you wouldn't have to."

But what about him, I want to ask. He had dreams before our parents died, and I know it was difficult, so difficult to keep it together. He never let on, though, just how hard it was. There are so many things I want to say to him, especially after crashing out in Chicago, but the words just won't come.

He comes to a stop on the main road and takes a left, his tires hitting the gravel that leads to the Grizzly River Ranch. It's been seven years since I came home. Seven years since I spent time at the big house. When I left, I never thought I'd come back. I'd told Truett I would see him again, but I hadn't planned on it. I'd seriously let the door hit me on the way out and flipped a middle finger to the ranch.

It was where I'd grown up, where I'd become an adult, but it was also the scene of the worst moments of my life.

Clearing my throat, I gaze over at him. "Every time we come over that hill, I think back to getting driven out here the day we found out about Mom and Dad. They brought me from the hospital, and once I saw the caution tape around the holding pen, I knew it wasn't a bad dream."

"Yeah," he inhales roughly, his nostrils flaring. "I see it every once in a while when I come over that hill too, but it's been better since we got rid of the pen."

I'm not sure it'll ever go away for me, but instead of admitting it, I give him a soft smile. "It is better since you did that. I'm sure it wasn't easy to look at it every day." Because he had. It'd still been up when I'd gone to college, and at least I'd been able to escape. Truett has never been able to do that. Within the blink of an eye, he became the owner of this ranch and my guardian.

He'd gone from being a teenager, about to be twenty years old, to the person in charge of all of this.

We hit a rut in the gravel, and I reach up to brace myself against the roof. "What's that over there?" I point to a new building behind the big house.

He grins widely. "That's Jesse's pride and joy. I'll have to let him explain it to you."

Jesse Nelson. God, I'd embarrassed myself with him the last time we saw one another. The thought of his name still brings heat to my face. "He's still working here?" I ask, my voice an octave higher.

A chuckle works its way out of his chest. "Yeah, you didn't think he was gonna go away just because you threw yourself at him, and he declined, did you?"

Teenage me had thought exactly that because she hadn't been able to imagine a reality in which I'd have to face him again. "Of course not. I'm just glad he's stayed loyal to you." I cover up my true thoughts.

"I mean, where else is he gonna go? He and I were pushed into the same situation, and he has a family of five to feed." Truett's expression softens slightly. "Jesse's been good to us, Aubs. Real good. When everything went to shit, he could've left for greener pastures, but he stayed. Helped me figure out how to run this place when I barely knew my ass from my elbow."

The guilt hits me like a punch to the gut. While I was off in Chicago, playing dress-up in my corporate world, Jesse was here helping my brother keep our family legacy alive. His parents and ours died together, best friends to the bitter end. "I'm glad he stayed," I say quietly, meaning it.

"He's got his own place now, just past the ridge. Built it

himself last year. But he's here most days, dawn to dusk." Truett glances at me sideways. "You two gonna be okay working together?"

Heat creeps up my neck. "Of course. We're adults now."

"Right." The skepticism in his voice is thick as molasses.

The truck bounces over another rut, and suddenly we're rounding the final bend. The big house comes into view, and my breath catches in my throat. It looks the same, but better—the wraparound porch has been painted a bright white, the red metal roof gleams, the sprawling oak tree out front, where I used to read for hours.

But it's not the same. Not really. Because the last time I saw this house, I was eighteen and broken, clutching an acceptance letter to Northwestern like it was my lifeline. I'd stood on that porch and sworn I'd never come back. Sworn I'd make something of myself in the big city and prove that I was more than just some ranch girl from South Dakota.

Look how that turned out.

Truett pulls up to the front of the house and kills the engine. For a moment, we just sit there in the sudden silence, dust settling around us like a shroud.

"You remember the night we got the call?" I ask quietly, my eyes fixed on the front door.

His hands tighten on the steering wheel. "Every damn day."

I was fifteen. Truett was nineteen, home from his first semester at State, full of plans and dreams about expanding the ranch, maybe even starting his own breeding program. We'd been watching some stupid movie in the living room when the phone rang. I can still hear the sound of Truett's voice changing, going from lazy and relaxed to sharp and focused in the span of a heartbeat.

"There's been an accident," he'd said after hanging up. "We need to get to the hospital."

But by the time we got there, it was too late. A drunk driver had hit their truck head-on coming home from their date night in Rapid City. Mom died on impact. Dad held on for two hours, but his injuries were too severe.

I'd spent that night in the hospital, numb and disbelieving, while Truett handled everything. The paperwork, the phone calls, the decisions that suddenly became his to make. When we finally came home the next morning, the house felt different. Empty. Like all the warmth had been sucked out of it.

"I used to hate this place," I admit, my voice barely above a whisper.

"I know." Truett's voice is rough. "Hell, I hated it too for a while. But it's home, Aubree. It's all we got left of them."

Before I can respond, the front door opens and someone steps onto the porch. My heart nearly stops.

Jesse Nelson.

He's not the lanky eighteen-year-old I remember. Seven years have filled him out in all the right places—broader shoulders, thicker arms, the kind of presence that commands attention without trying. His dark hair is longer now, curling slightly at the edges where it meets his collar, and there's a beard covering his jaw that definitely wasn't there when I left.

But his eyes are the same. That deep brown that always made me feel like he could see right through me.

"About time you got back," he calls out, his voice carrying

that familiar hint of amusement. "I was starting to think you'd gotten lost."

Truett snorts. "Jesse, you remember my sister, Aubree."

As if he could forget. As if any of us could forget the night of my graduation party, when I'd cornered him by the barn and kissed him like my life depended on it. When I'd whispered against his lips that I was eighteen now, that I'd always had feelings for him, that maybe we could...

"Welcome home, Aubree," Jesse says, and there's something in his tone that makes me wonder if he's thinking about that night too.

I force myself to get out of the truck, my legs feeling unsteady on gravel I haven't felt in years. "Hey, Jesse." I aim for casual, but my voice comes out breathy and uncertain.

He's walking toward us now, and I can see the changes of time up close. There are lines around his eyes from squinting in the sun, and his hands are rougher, probably more calloused than I remember. He's wearing a simple white T-shirt and faded jeans, but somehow he makes it look like he stepped off the cover of a romance novel.

"You look good," he says, his eyes looking me up and down. I hate the way my pulse quickens at the compliment.

"Thanks." I tuck a strand of hair behind my ear, suddenly self-conscious about my wrinkled clothes. "You look...different."

"Seven years'll do that to a person." His smile is easy, but there's something guarded in his eyes. "Heard you were doing big things in Chicago."

"Yeah, well." I shrug, trying to play it off, like it doesn't mean as much as it does. "Big things have a way of falling apart."

Truett clears his throat, breaking the moment. "Jesse, can you help me get her stuff?"

"Sure thing." Jesse moves to the back of the truck, and I catch a whiff of his scent, something woody and masculine that makes my stomach flip.

God, I'm pathetic. Seven years away, and I'm still reacting to him like a teenager with a crush.

But I'm not a teenager anymore. I'm a twenty-five-year-old woman who just had her entire life implode spectacularly. I came home to lick my wounds and figure out my next move, not to moon over my brother's best friend.

Even if he does look like he stepped out of my most vivid fantasies.

"I'll show you to your new room," Truett says, shouldering my larger suitcase. "Then we can talk about what you want to do tomorrow."

I nod, following him toward the house. But as we climb the porch steps, I can feel Jesse's eyes on me, and I can't help but wonder if coming home was the best idea after all.

Because some feelings, it seems, are harder to outrun than others.

And some mistakes have a way of following you home.

TWO
JESSE

SHE'S EXACTLY as I remember her, only hotter. No longer the girl I had to let down easy. Instead, she's the woman I could have if given the chance, and make no mistake, I could still have her. Especially with the way she was eyeing me. But I have to remember now, this isn't just my best friend's little sister. It could have much bigger implications.

Groaning and shaking my head, I go over to where her other suitcase is stacked. It's not nearly as big as I thought it would be, but I have a feeling there's more coming. She's always been high-maintenance, and I don't foresee that changing anytime soon.

With a grunt, I heft it up and head into the house, stopping when I hear my name.

"Jesse, want us to ride out to the south field?" It's my brother Carson, the youngest of the bunch. The one who needs the most instruction and micromanaging. He'll learn how to make decisions on his own at some point. At least, that's what I keep telling myself.

"Yeah, go check fences. I'll come join you later," I say as I give him a look.

He reads it and nods. "See ya."

I watch Carson jog toward the barn, his boots kicking up dust with each step.

The screen door creaks as I push through it, the familiar sound echoing through the ranch house. This place hasn't changed much since we were kids running through these same halls. Hell, I can still see the scuff marks on the hardwood floor from when Truett, Aubree, and I would slide around in our socks after Sunday dinner. Our parents were best friends, and we spent more time here than we did at our own ranch. It still stands that way.

"Upstairs, second door on the right," Truett calls from the kitchen, not bothering to look up from whatever he's tinkering with at the table. Looks like part of the irrigation system from the back pasture. There's a small piece bent, and he's determined to get it fixed. Up here, people don't bother him all the time.

I take the stairs two at a time, muscle memory guiding me to what used to be Aubree's room. The door's already open, and I can see she's started making herself at home. A few things are scattered on the bed—some fancy-looking clothes that probably cost more than most people around here make in a month. It's not like she's going to be wearing them here anytime soon.

Setting the suitcase down by the window, I can't help but look around. Truett kept it exactly the same as when she left. Purple walls with those ridiculous boy band posters she used to obsess over. The bookshelf is still packed with romance novels she thought no one knew she was reading. I knew, though.

Caught her more than once, completely absorbed in some story about cowboys and love and happy endings.

The irony isn't lost on me.

"Jesse?" Her voice floats up from downstairs, and I feel that familiar tightening in my chest. The same one I was fighting all those years ago when she left.

"Up here," I call back, heading toward the stairs.

She's standing at the bottom of the stairs, looking up at me with those green eyes that have haunted more dreams than I care to admit. Her hair's longer now, falling in waves past her shoulders, and she's wearing jeans that hug her curves in ways that should be illegal.

"Thanks for bringing that up," she says, tucking a strand of hair behind her ear. It's a nervous habit she's had since we were kids.

"No problem." I stop a few steps from the bottom, causing us not to be too far apart. Big mistake. This close, I can smell her perfume–something expensive and floral that's nothing like the cheap drugstore stuff she used to wear in high school.

"Truett!" The front door slams, and heavy footsteps echo through the house. "That damn cultivator's acting up again. I need you to come take a look."

It's Dave, our foreman of the crop side of things. Good timing, because the tension between Aubree and me is thick enough to cut with a knife.

Truett appears from the kitchen, wiping grease off his hands with an old rag. "What's it doing now?"

"Same thing as last month. Keeps jamming up on the left side."

"All right, let me grab my tools." Truett disappears back into the kitchen, then returns with his toolbox. He pauses, glancing between Aubree and me. "Don't kill each other while I'm gone. Behave yourselves."

If only he knew how loaded that statement is.

The door closes behind them, and suddenly the house feels too small. Aubree and I are alone for the first time since she left South Dakota.

"So," she says, shifting her weight from one foot to the other. "This is awkward."

I laugh, but there's no humor in it. "That's one word for it."

She moves toward the living room, and I follow, keeping what I hope is a safe distance. She settles onto the couch, the same couch where I used to help her with her math homework while trying not to notice how her lips moved when she concentrated.

"What made you come back?" I ask, choosing the chair across from her instead of sitting beside her. Smart move, Jesse.

Her smile falters, and for a second, I see a crack in that polished exterior she's been wearing since she got out of the truck. "I needed to lick my wounds, I guess. My life didn't exactly work out the way I envisioned it."

There's pain in her voice, real pain, and my first instinct is to comfort her. But I hold back. I've learned the hard way that getting too close to Aubree Weber only leads to a hard cock and a feeling of being unsatisfied.

"Maybe you needed to be humbled," I say, and immediately regret the harshness in my tone.

Her head snaps up, brown eyes flashing. "Excuse me?"

"You heard me." I lean forward, resting my elbows on my knees. "Before you left, Truett gave you everything you wanted to make up for your parents being gone. You were spoiled rotten, Aubree. You always have been."

She stands up so fast the couch cushion bounces. "You don't know anything about my life, Jesse. You don't know what I've been through."

"I know you left here to lick your wounds because I turned you down. I know the bright lights of Chicago were way too enticing for you to ignore them. I know you barely called or visited. I know Truett worried himself sick about you for years. He stayed here, along with me, killing himself to make sure you didn't worry, while he took it all within himself."

"That's not fair, and you know it." Her voice is rising, color flooding her cheeks. "I was eighteen years old. I wanted to see the world, experience things. I'd lost my parents, and they weren't able to take that cruise they wanted to. They never got to visit New York City. Wanting to make memories before I die doesn't make me a spoiled brat."

"Doesn't it?" I stand too, and suddenly we're facing each other across the coffee table like opponents in a boxing ring. "You had everything handed to you on a silver platter, and it still wasn't enough. We weren't enough."

"God, I hate that you think you know me so well." She's pacing now, hands gesturing wildly. "You think because we grew up together, because you're Truett's best friend, that gives you the right to judge every decision I've made?"

"I'm not judging..."

"Yes, you are!" She spins to face me, and there are tears in her eyes now. "You've been judging me since the day I left. Hell, you were judging me before I left. I could see it in your eyes that night...that night when I..."

She trails off, but I know exactly what night she's talking about. Her eighteenth birthday. The night that everything changed between us.

"Say it," I challenge, taking a step around the coffee table.

"No."

"Say it, Aubree."

"Fine!" The word explodes out of her. "That night I kissed you, okay? Are you happy now? That stupid, meaningless kiss that obviously meant nothing to you."

Something inside me snaps. "Meaningless?"

"Yes, meaningless. God, I wish you weren't my first kiss. I wish I'd saved it for someone who actually..."

I don't let her finish. Before I can think better of it, I'm across that distance, my hand wrapping around her throat. Not hard enough to hurt, but firm enough to stop her retreat.

"Don't." My voice is low, dangerous.

"Let go of me, Jesse."

Instead, I take another step forward, backing her up until she hits the wall beside the fireplace. My free hand comes up to brace against the wall next to her head, caging her in.

"You may wish you could take it back," I say, my face inches from hers. "But you'd never forget it. And neither would I."

Her breath hitches, and I can feel the rapid rise and fall of her chest where it almost touches mine.

"That kiss," I continue, my voice barely above a whisper. "Sometimes still keeps me up at night."

The admission hangs between us like the discharge of a loaded gun. I can see the shock in her eyes, followed quickly by something else. Something that looks a lot like the want I've been fighting for years.

"Jesse..." She breathes, and my name on her lips is almost my undoing.

I should step back. I should let her go and walk away and pretend this conversation never happened. Instead, I lean closer until I can feel the warmth radiating from her skin.

"You want to know the truth, Aubree? That kiss ruined me for anyone else. Every woman I've been with since then, I've compared to you. To that one perfect moment when you looked at me like I was everything you'd ever wanted."

Her eyes flutter closed, and I can see the pulse jumping in her throat.

"But you left," I continue, my thumb unconsciously stroking across the delicate skin of her throat. "You left, and you took that moment with you. So don't you dare stand there and tell me it was meaningless."

When she opens her eyes, they're bright with unshed tears. "I never knew," she whispers.

"How could you? You were so busy planning your escape from this place, from me, that you never looked back long enough to see what you left behind."

"That's not...I didn't leave because of you."

"Didn't you?" I search her face, looking for the truth. "Because it sure felt like it. One day, you were talking about going to college in Rapid City, maybe studying business, so you could help run the ranch. The next day, after that kiss, you were applying to schools in Chicago, and leaving on the off chance that one of them accepted you."

She tries to pull away, but I don't let her. "That's not why I left."

"Then why?"

"Because I was scared!" The words burst out of her like a dam breaking. "I was scared of how you made me feel. I was scared that if I stayed, I'd never be anything more than Truett's little sister who had a crush on his best friend. I was scared that you'd break my heart, and I'd have to see you every day for the rest of my life. I was terrified that I'd spend my whole life pining for something that was never going to happen, and I'd end up regretting it if I lost my life in a freak crash with a drunk driver."

The fight goes out of me all at once. I release her throat and step back, running a hand through my hair. "So you broke mine instead."

She slides down the wall slightly, looking suddenly fragile. "I didn't know. I swear, Jesse. I didn't know."

"Well, now you do."

We stand there in silence, the weight of years of unspoken words settling between us. Outside, I can hear the distant sound of machinery, reminding me that the world is still turning despite the fact that mine just shifted on its axis.

"I should go," I say finally. "Truett will be back soon."

She nods, not meeting my eyes. "Okay."

I make it to the front door before she speaks again.

"Jesse?"

I pause, my hand on the doorknob, but I don't turn around.

"I'm sorry," she says softly. "For leaving the way I did. For hurting you. I never meant to."

I close my eyes, fighting the urge to go back to her. "I know."

Then I'm outside, the late afternoon sun blinding after the dimness of the house. I take a deep breath of fresh air, trying to clear my head, but all I can smell is her perfume clinging to my shirt.

This is bad. This is very, very bad.

Carson's riding back from the south pasture, and he waves when he sees me. I wave back, grateful for the distraction.

"How'd the fences look?" I call out as he approaches.

"Good. Found a couple of loose posts near the creek, but nothing major." He swings down from his horse, studying my face with the kind of perception that runs in our family. "You okay? You look like you've seen a ghost."

If only it were that simple.

"I'm fine," I lie. "Just tired."

He doesn't look convinced, but he doesn't push it either. "Want me to take care of Ranger?" he asks, nodding toward my horse, who's still saddled and waiting by the barn.

"Yeah, thanks."

I watch him lead both horses toward the barn, then head for my truck. I need to get out of here before Truett gets back and starts asking questions I can't answer.

But as I drive down the dusty road away from the ranch, I can't shake the image of Aubree pressed against that wall, looking at me like maybe, just maybe, she wants me as much as I've always wanted her.

THREE
AUBREE

THAT KISS STILL KEEPS *me up at night.* I never thought I'd hear those words from him. Never thought that stupid kiss the night I turned eighteen even mattered to him. It'd mattered to me, obviously. But I'd never gotten any indication that he'd felt anything.

God, coming back here is going to open up so many boxes I've closed tight and shoved into the recesses of my mind that it might as well kill me.

One good thing, though, is connecting with my high school best friend, Nora. We've FaceTimed, emailed, texted, and she's even visited me, but we haven't lived in the same city since I left.

I pull out my phone and scroll to her contact, my fingers still slightly shaky from my encounter with Jesse.

A
I'm home!

Immediately, there are three dots.

N
Oh my god! I'm so excited. Wanna hang out?

Looking at the stuff around my room, I decide quickly I don't want to spend my first afternoon and evening unpacking. There's plenty of time for that. Besides, I need a distraction from replaying Jesse's words over and over in my mind.

A
Yes! Come get me?

N
I'm over at the vet's office. I'll be there in fifteen.

A
See ya!

Nora's a vet tech who helps out through the county, and I'm lucky she's close. Quickly, I change, trading my travel clothes for a comfortable pair of jeans and a T-shirt, and wash the travel off me, before grabbing my purse and heading downstairs to wait on the porch.

The wooden steps creak under my feet as I settle onto the top step, just like they used to when I was a kid waiting for my dad to drive me to the bus stop. Some things never change, I suppose. The prairie stretches out before me, endless and golden under the late afternoon sun. It's beautiful in a way I'd forgotten, or maybe chose to forget when I was desperate to escape to what I thought were bigger and better things.

"Already going somewhere?" Truett asks. He's standing in the doorway, thumbing through his cell phone, probably checking the weather forecast like he does every few hours during every season of the year.

"Yeah, Nora's coming to get me. We're gonna catch up. Is that okay with you, Dad?"

The word slips out before I can stop it. I haven't called him Dad since I was sixteen and trying to assert my independence. His expression softens, and I see a flash of the boy who turned into a man in one night and chased away the monsters from my nightmares.

He snorts, but it's gentle. "It's fine. If you need a ride, because I know how the two of you get, call me."

With those words, it's like I never left. Nora and I had been notorious for losing track of time, getting caught up in whatever adventure we'd dreamed up. There was the time we decided to hike to the old mining cave and didn't come back until after midnight, or when we got distracted by a roadside farmer's market and came home with three pies and a goat we'd somehow convinced Truett to let us keep for exactly one week.

"Love you, Tru."

"Yeah, yeah. I gotta go. Be safe, okay?"

I watch him walk toward the barn where Dave's probably still fighting with that cultivator, his shoulders set in the determined line that means he won't stop until whatever's broken is fixed. He's always been that way—a problem solver, a fixer. It's probably why he's taken care of everyone around him his whole life, including me.

The guilt hits me like a physical blow. Jesse was right, wasn't he? I had been spoiled. Truett gave me everything after our parents died, tried to be mother and father both, and I repaid him by running away the first chance I got.

A cloud of dust on the horizon signals Nora's approach, and I push the guilty thoughts aside. There'll be time for self-deprecation later. Right now, I need my best friend and whatever normalcy she can provide.

Nora's truck, newer than the old one she drove in high school, skids to a stop beside me. Grizzly River Vet Services is slapped on the door, which reminds me that we've all grown up. Through the windshield, I can see her grinning like a maniac, her red hair pulled back in a messy bun that somehow looks effortlessly chic on her.

"Aubree Michelle!" she shouts, pulling out my middle name, jumping out of the truck before it's fully stopped. "Get your ass over here and hug me!"

I can't help but laugh as I run down the steps and into her arms. She smells like hay and the vanilla body spray she's worn since we were fifteen. It's the smell of home in a way that's different from the ranch house but just as powerful.

"God, I missed you," I mumble into her shoulder.

"Missed you too, city girl." She pulls back to look at me, her hands on my shoulders. "You look like you're doing okay."

Okay is a good way to put it. I'm not good, not bad, but I'm making it. "I am."

She links her arm through mine, steering me toward the truck. "Come on. Let's get out of here before your brother decides he wants to interrogate us about where we're going, and then tells us it's a bad idea."

"He's not that bad," I protest, but I'm already climbing into the passenger seat.

"Please. Remember when we were seventeen, and we wanted to go to that party at Miller's pond? He made you promise to text him every hour and had Jesse follow us in his truck."

The mention of Jesse's name sends a flutter through my stomach. "I forgot about that."

"I didn't. Jesse parked where he thought we couldn't see him and spent the whole night glaring at any guy who looked at you sideways." She starts the truck and backs out of the driveway, gravel crunching under the tires. "Looking back, it was kind of sweet. At the time, I wanted to murder him."

"He was just looking out for me because Truett asked him to." The words sound hollow even to me.

Nora gives me a look that clearly says she's not buying it. "Sure, he was. That's why he looked like he wanted to commit actual homicide when Brad Patterson asked you to dance."

I remember that night. I remember Jesse cutting in after one song, his hand warm and steady on my back as he guided me away from Brad and toward the bonfire. I remember thinking he was being overprotective and annoying. Now I wonder if there was more to it. Did he like me back then, when I was quietly pining over him?

"Anyway," Nora continues, turning onto the main road toward town. "Enough about ancient history. How are you feeling about being back?"

"Honestly? I'm not sure. It's weird being in my old room, seeing everything exactly the same. Part of me expected things to change more, you know?"

"Time moves differently here," she says, and there's wisdom in her voice that I'd forgotten about. Nora always was the philosophical one. "But you've changed. I can see it more now that you're back in Grizzly River. It wasn't so apparent when I visited you in Chicago."

"How?"

She's quiet for a moment, considering. "You're more... polished, I guess. Like you've learned how to hide parts of yourself. The Aubree I knew wore her heart on her sleeve."

Her words hit uncomfortably close to home. "Maybe that's a good thing. Maybe I needed to learn how to protect myself."

"Maybe. Or maybe you just got hurt and learned to build walls."

She knows more about what happened than anyone else.

I turn to look out the window at the passing landscape—fields of corn and wheat, the occasional farmhouse, cattle dotting the pastures like brown and black specks against the green. It's peaceful in a way Chicago never was, but it also feels confining, like the whole world could be contained within these county lines.

"So where are we going?" I ask, deflecting from her too-accurate observations.

"My place. I have an apartment above the hardware store in Grizzly River now. It's tiny, but it's mine. I thought we could grab lunch at the diner and then catch up properly."

Grizzly River is barely big enough to be called a town. One main street with a handful of businesses and maybe three hundred people if you're being generous. But it has charm, with its old brick buildings and tree-lined streets. It's the kind of place where everyone knows everyone, and secrets are impossible to keep.

The diner looks exactly the same as it did in high school, complete with red vinyl booths and a black-and-white checkered floor that's probably older than both of us. Marge Henderson is still behind the counter, her gray hair teased high and her apron stained with what looks like gravy.

"Well, I'll be damned," Marge says when she sees me. "Aubree Weber, as I live and breathe. Heard you were coming home."

News travels fast in small towns. "Hi, Mrs. Henderson. Good to see you."

"You too, honey. You look good. City life's been treating you well."

If only she knew. "Thank you."

"What can I get you girls?"

We order—a chicken salad sandwich and sweet tea for me, a burger and fries for Nora—and find a booth in the back where we can talk without the entire diner listening in.

"Okay," Nora says once Marge has brought our drinks. "Spill. And don't give me the sanitized version you gave me last time I asked. I want the real story of why you're back."

I take a sip of sweet tea, buying myself time. It's perfect, exactly the right balance of sweet and bitter, nothing like the fancy drinks I've gotten used to in Chicago.

"My life imploded," I say finally.

"How so?"

"Remember how I always said I wanted to work in marketing? Have a career, be independent, all that?"

She nods.

"Well, I got what I wanted. You and I never really talked about it, but the job I had? It was great. I had a nice apartment, friends. I thought I was living the dream."

"But?"

"But the man I told you I was completely in love with? The one I was seeing, and I was so excited about?"

"I do. We didn't talk about it much because you didn't want to, and I wanted to respect that," she says, taking another bite of her food.

I put my drink down. "I found out he was married."

Nora's eyes widen. "Oh shit."

"Yeah. Oh shit is right." I lean back against the vinyl seat, the memories still sharp enough to hurt. "His name was Daniel. He was a senior account manager, older, sophisticated. Everything I thought I wanted in a man."

"How long were you actually together?"

"Eight months. Eight months of thinking I'd finally found my person, you know? He was charming and funny, and he made me feel like I was the most important thing in his world."

Marge brings our food, and I wait until she's out of earshot before continuing.

"We kept it quiet at work, company policy and all that. I thought he was being professional. Turns out he was just being careful not to let his wife find out."

"Jesus, Aubree. How did you find out?"

I take a bite of my sandwich, chewing slowly while I work up the courage to tell the story I've been trying not to think about for weeks.

"Company party. He'd been acting weird all week, distant. I thought maybe he was planning to go public with our relationship, make some grand gesture. You know, like the ones in romance novels. I was so naïve." I laugh, but there's no humor in it. "I showed up in this gorgeous dress, ready to be his date officially for the first time."

"And?"

"And he was there with his wife. Very pregnant wife. Like, ready-to-pop pregnant." The memory still makes my stomach clench. "She was beautiful, Nora. Sweet and glowing and everything a pregnant woman should be. And she kept talking about how excited they were about the baby, how Daniel was going to be such a good father."

Nora reaches across the table and squeezes my hand. "That bastard."

"The worst part was, he saw me see them. And he had the audacity to look guilty. Not ashamed or apologetic. Guilty. Like I was the one who'd done something wrong by showing up at a work function."

"What did you do?"

"I went to the bathroom and threw up. Then I went home, packed a bag, and spent the weekend at a hotel trying to figure out what the hell I was going to do with my life. I didn't want him to be able to find me. So I made it where he couldn't."

"Did you confront him?"

"Monday morning. He actually tried to explain it away, said it was complicated, that he and his wife were having problems. All the classic cheater lines." I push lettuce around on my plate, my appetite gone. "I told him exactly what I thought of him and his complications, then I went to HR."

"Good for you."

"Not really. Turns out, reporting the married head of the

accounting department for having an affair with you is a great way to make your work life unbearable. Suddenly, I was getting the worst assignments, being left out of meetings, and generally frozen out by everyone who mattered."

Nora's expression darkens. "That's illegal, isn't it?"

"Probably. But proving it would have been a nightmare, and I just...I didn't have the fight left in me. I'd spent eight months thinking I was building a life with someone, only to find out I was just a side piece. It broke something in me."

We sit in silence for a moment, the sounds of the diner washing over us.

"So you quit?" Nora asks finally.

"I quit. Cashed out my 401k, broke my lease, and came home to lick my wounds." I meet her eyes across the table. "Pathetic, right?"

"Not pathetic. Human." She leans forward, her expression fierce. "That asshole used you, Aubree. He lied to you for eight months. You have every right to be hurt and angry and confused."

"I keep thinking I should have known. There had to be signs, right? Nobody's that good at compartmentalizing their life."

"Or maybe he was just a really good liar. Sociopaths usually are." She gives me a wink.

That makes me smile for the first time since we sat down. This is why, after everything, she's still one of my best friends. "Thanks for not saying 'I told you so.'"

"About what?"

"About leaving here in the first place. About thinking I was too good for small-town life. About being a spoiled brat who didn't appreciate what she had."

Nora's eyebrows shoot up. "Who called you a spoiled brat?"

Heat floods my cheeks. "Jesse."

"Ah." Understanding dawns in her eyes. "You've talked to him already."

"If you can call it talking. It was more like him listing all my character flaws while I tried not to cry."

"What exactly did he say?"

I give her the abbreviated version of our confrontation, leaving out the part about him grabbing my throat and the admission about our kiss keeping him up at night. Some things are too raw to share, even with my best friend.

"He's not wrong," I say when I finish. "I was spoiled. Truett did give me everything I wanted, and I did take it for granted."

"Maybe. But you were also eighteen and grieving and trying to figure out who you were outside of this place. That doesn't make you a brat. It makes you normal."

"Then why do I feel so guilty about it?"

"Because you have a conscience. Which, for the record, spoiled brats usually don't."

Marge refills our tea glasses without being asked, a small kindness that reminds me why I used to love this place.

"Can I ask you something?" Nora says once Marge is gone.

"Sure."

"Was this Daniel guy anything like Jesse?"

The question catches me off guard. "What do you mean?"

"I mean, was he tall and dark and brooding? Did he have that whole strong, silent type thing going on?"

I think about it, really think about it. Daniel was tall, yes. Dark hair, yes. But brooding? Not exactly. He was more...

polished. Smooth. He knew exactly what to say and when to say it, how to make me feel special and wanted.

Jesse's never been smooth in that way. He's blunt and honest and sometimes cruel in his directness. But he's also real in a way Daniel never was. I've always thought I could fix Jesse if he'd only just give me a chance.

"Not really," I say finally.

"Hmm."

"What's that supposed to mean?"

"Nothing. Just...hmm."

I know that look. It's the same one she used to get in high school when she was formulating a theory about why our chemistry teacher wore the same tie every Tuesday or why the quarterback always ate lunch alone on Fridays.

"Nora."

"I'm just saying, it's interesting that you spent something like seven years trying to get over Jesse Nelson and ended up with a guy who was the complete opposite of him."

"I wasn't trying to get over Jesse. There was nothing to get over."

She gives me a look that clearly says she thinks I'm delusional.

"There wasn't," I insist. "We kissed once. Once. And then I left for college. End of story."

"If you say so."

"I do say so."

But even as I say the words, I can feel Jesse's hand on my throat, can hear his voice saying that kiss still keeps him up at night. And I wonder if maybe, just maybe, I've been lying to myself for all these years.

We finish lunch and walk the two blocks to Nora's apartment, the late afternoon sun warm on our shoulders. Grizzly River is quiet at this time of day. Most people are still at work or tending to their ranches. It's peaceful in a way that makes me understand why Nora chose to stay.

Her apartment is small but cozy, with exposed brick walls and wide-plank floors that probably date back to when the building was first constructed. She's decorated it with a mix of vintage finds and modern touches that somehow work together perfectly.

"This is really nice," I say, running my hand along the back of her couch.

"Thanks. It's not much, but it's mine. Want some wine? I have a bottle of that Moscato we had last time I visited you."

"God, yes. Please."

She disappears into the kitchen, leaving me to explore. The walls are covered with photos—some of us from high school, some of her family, some of her with various animals she's helped over the years. There's one of her with a horse that looks vaguely familiar.

"Is this Thunder?" I call out, pointing to the photo.

"Yep. Took that last month. He's doing well, by the way. Still ornery as hell, but healthy."

Thunder was my horse growing up, a cantankerous old gelding who only liked me and Truett. When I left for college, I'd assumed Truett would sell him, but apparently, he'd just moved him to a different pasture.

"I should go see him," I say when Nora returns with two glasses of wine.

"You should. He's at the Hendersons' place now. They

board horses for people who can't keep them on their own land anymore."

We settle onto her couch, and she tucks her feet under her like she used to do during our marathon movie nights in high school.

"Okay," she says, "I told you about my boring life. Now I want details about yours. The real details."

"What do you want to know?"

"Do you miss it?"

So I tell her. There were things I loved, but there were also other things. I talk about my life. About my work friends, who were fun to grab drinks with but never became real friends. About the dates that never went anywhere because I was too busy comparing everyone to a memory I couldn't quite shake.

"You were homesick," she says when I finish.

"No, I wasn't. I was just...adjusting."

"For years?"

"It takes time to build a life somewhere new."

"Or you were trying to build a life somewhere that never felt like home."

I want to argue with her, but the wine and the familiar comfort of her friendship are making it hard to maintain my defenses.

"Maybe," I admit. "Maybe I was running from something instead of running to something."

"And now you're back."

"Now I'm back."

"For how long?"

It's the question I've been avoiding, even in my own mind. "I don't know. Long enough to figure out what comes next, I guess."

"And what if what comes next is staying?"

The idea should terrify me. Six weeks ago, the thought of moving back to South Dakota permanently would have sent me into a panic. But sitting here, in this quiet apartment in this tiny town, surrounded by the easy comfort of old friendship, it doesn't seem like the worst thing in the world.

"I guess we'll see," I say.

And for the first time since I got Daniel's wife's pregnancy announcement in my face, I actually mean it.

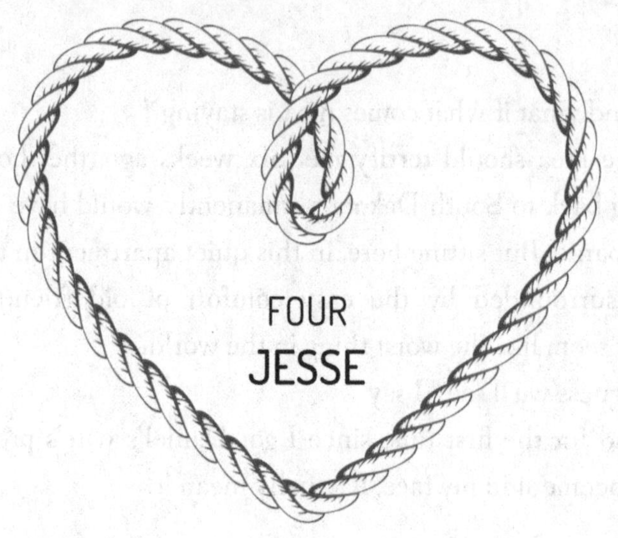

FOUR
JESSE

IT'S FUCKING DUSTY TODAY. We need rain in a bad way, which is why I have the guys going to check fences. I'm afraid some of the old posts will dry rot, and then we'll be chasing cattle, while potentially losing money.

I take my job as Truett's right-hand man seriously. We've been doing this together since our parents died, and we've had to do a good portion of it by the skin of our teeth. There were no life insurance policies, and we had siblings to take care of.

No matter what that meant.

I push the bandana up higher over my nose to keep the dust from choking me, and press my knees against my horse, urging it to go faster. Within minutes, I'm cresting a hill and see my brother, along with a few other men, doing what I asked.

"How's everything lookin' up here?" I ask when I get close enough for them to be able to hear me.

Carson nods toward two obviously brand-new posts.

"Couple need replacing. We can hold off on most of 'em, though."

"Sounds good." I motion for him to follow me as I ride my horse over to the side so that we can have a private conversation.

"What's up?" he questions.

I glance back at the other men, making sure they're still focused on their work, before turning my attention back to Carson. The afternoon sun beats down mercilessly, and I can feel sweat mixing with dust under my shirt. This conversation needs to happen now, while we have the cover of legitimate ranch work.

"We got business tonight," I say, keeping my voice low. "Devlin's expecting us at the usual spot around midnight." I mention our oldest brother.

Carson's jaw tightens, and he shifts in his saddle. "What kind of business?"

"The kind that keeps food on the table and this ranch running." I pull out a worn piece of paper from my shirt pocket, unfolding it carefully. "There's a shipment coming through on the old county road. Easy pickup, minimal risk."

My brother studies the crude map I've sketched, his green eyes, so similar to mine, narrowing as he takes in the details. "How minimal are we talking?"

"Single driver, no escort. Devlin's got inside information that it's carrying enough to cover our expenses for the next three months." I fold the paper back up, tucking it away. "We'll be in and out before anyone knows what happened."

Carson rubs his beard, a nervous habit he's had since we were teenagers. "And Truett?"

"Truett stays home." The words come out harder than I

intended. "He's got Aubree to think about now. Can't risk her getting suspicious or, worse, getting involved. That's what Devlin's there for." Many would say that he should've been the one to take control of the family, but the truth is, I've always been the strongest of the bunch.

"She's not stupid, Jesse. She's gonna notice if we start acting different."

I know he's right. Aubree always was too observant for her own good, even as a kid. Those deep brown eyes of hers see everything, file it away, piece it together like some kind of puzzle. It's part of what makes her so damn appealing and so damn dangerous to what we do.

"That's why we keep things normal for the next week or so," I explain. "We do our regular work, act like nothing's changed. Tonight's job gets done quietly and clean. Nobody gets hurt, nobody traces anything back to us."

The wind picks up, sending another cloud of dust swirling around us. I pull my bandana back up, watching as the other men continue their work on the fence line. From a distance, we probably look like two brothers discussing ranch business. Nothing suspicious about that.

"What about the other guys?" Carson nods toward the workers. "They gonna ask questions if we disappear tonight?"

"Already handled. Told them we're riding out early to check the south pasture. They'll think we're just being thorough." I pause, letting the lie settle. "Far as anyone knows, we're just doing our jobs."

Carson's horse shifts restlessly beneath him, picking up on his rider's tension. "This is getting risky, Jesse. We've been lucky for years, but eventually luck runs out."

"You think I don't know that?" The words snap out before I can stop them. I take a breath, forcing myself to calm down. Carson's just being cautious, which is smart. "Look, I know it's dangerous. But what choice do we have? The ranch barely breaks even on good years, and this hasn't been a good year."

"There're always choices."

"Yeah? Like what? Sell the land our parents died trying to keep? We all know that wreck was more than a drunk driver who crossed the yellow line. Let the bank take everything they worked for?" I shake my head. "Not happening. Not while I'm still breathing."

The silence stretches between us, filled only by the sound of hammers on fence posts and the distant lowing of cattle. Carson knows I'm right, even if he doesn't like it. We've had this conversation before, in different variations, but it always comes back to the same thing: we do what we have to do to survive.

"Tell me about tonight," he says finally.

I outline the plan, keeping my voice low and my eyes on the horizon. The shipment will be traveling light, just a single truck with unbranded cattle, which makes them easier to steal. We'll intercept it at the old bridge where the county road crosses Miller's Creek. It's isolated, far from any houses or main roads. Perfect for our purposes.

"We'll need masks," I continue. "And Carson? No names. Even if something goes wrong, even if we get separated, no names."

He nods grimly. "Understood."

"Devlin's handling the disposal of the truck and trailer. We take the cattle and put them in our trailer. By morning, we're just two cowboys who spent the night checking cattle."

The plan is solid, as solid as these things ever are. But there's always that element of unpredictability, that moment when everything can go sideways. I've learned to live with that fear, to push it down and focus on what needs to be done.

"What about weapons?" Carson asks.

"Just sidearms. This isn't supposed to be violent. We want them scared, not dead." I pause, meeting his eyes. "But if things go bad..."

"I know."

Of course he knows. We've been down this road before, more times than I care to count. Sometimes I wonder what our parents would think if they could see us now. Would they understand? Would they hate what we've become?

I shake off those thoughts. No point in dwelling on ghosts and regrets. The dead don't have to worry about keeping the lights on or putting food on the table. The living do.

"We meet at the old barn at eleven," I tell him. "That gives us time to get in position without rushing."

Carson nods, then glances back at the other workers. "Should we head back? They'll start wondering if we disappear for too long."

"Yeah." I gather my reins, preparing to rejoin the group. "Carson?"

"Yeah?"

"Remember what I said about Aubree. She can't know about this. About any of it. That's important to me and Truett."

His expression darkens. "You really think she'd turn us in?"

"I think she's got a conscience. And sometimes that's more dangerous than any enemy." I pause, choosing my words carefully. "She cares about right and wrong in a way we can't afford to anymore."

"She cares about us too."

"I know. That's what makes it complicated."

We ride back to rejoin the work crew, falling into the familiar rhythm of ranch life. But underneath the normalcy, I can feel the tension coiling in my chest. Tonight will either solve our problems for the next few months or create new ones we can't imagine.

As the afternoon wears on, I find myself thinking about Aubree more than I should. The way she looked when I had her pressed up against the wall. The way her honey-blonde hair caught the light when she turned her head. The way her lips curved when she smiled.

She's dangerous to our operation, but she's also the reason I keep doing this. Her, and Truett, and the legacy our parents left behind. Everything I do, every risk I take—it's all for family.

Even if they never know the full price I'm willing to pay.

The sun starts its descent toward the horizon, painting the sky in shades of orange and red. In a few hours, Carson, Devlin, and I will be riding out into the darkness, putting everything on the line once again. But right now, in this moment, we're just cowboys fixing a fence on a dusty ranch.

Sometimes, the lie is easier to live with than the truth.

FIVE
AUBREE

"THANKS FOR DROPPING ME OFF," I tell Nora as we come to a stop in front of the big house. "I didn't expect to be out as late as we were, but it was fun. I missed you."

She smiles over at me. "I missed you too. You'll have to join me for girls' night out on Friday. We have a really good time."

She mentioned this earlier tonight. "I know most of the girls from high school, don't I?"

"You do, and they'd all love to see you."

There's still a part of me that feels weird about being home. Like, I came back because I failed, when that's not right. I was lied to, my heart was broken, and I didn't have a choice. "We'll see. I'll let you know for sure Thursday?"

"Take your time. Ain't like it's going anywhere. Talk to ya later."

I get out and wave goodbye to her. Truett's truck is parked next to the barn, and the light is on in his window. It'd be easy to go inside and talk to him, but it's not what I want to do. Instead, I walk to the back porch and have a seat on the old swing that's been here for decades. Testing it out, I bounce slightly to make sure it can hold my weight, and when I'm sure it can, I give a push with my toe. Looking out over the backside of our property, I can't help but be proud Truett has been able to keep it for as long as he has.

I've been sitting in the silence, except for the sounds of the night around the ranch, when I hear the definite sound of riders on horseback approaching.

The rhythmic sound of hoofbeats grows louder, and I strain my eyes to see through the darkness. Two riders emerge from the shadows, and even in the dim light, I recognize the familiar silhouettes. Jesse and Devlin, riding side by side like they have since we were kids.

But something feels off. It's well past midnight, far too late for routine ranch work. The way they're sitting in their saddles doesn't match the casual pace of men finishing up a normal day.

They pull up near the barn, and I watch Jesse dismount with that fluid grace he's always had. Even from this distance, I can make out the sharp lines of his profile, the way his dark hair falls across his forehead under his hat. My heart does that stupid flutter thing it's been doing since I came home, the same reaction I had to him when I was seventeen and thought I knew everything about love.

"Hey there," I call out, trying to keep my voice light and casual.

Both men turn toward the porch, and I see Jesse's shoulders relax slightly when he spots me. "Aubree. Didn't expect to see you out here this late."

I push off with my toe again, setting the swing in motion.

"Could say the same about you two. What were you doing out there in the dark?"

There's a pause, just long enough to make me suspicious. Jesse exchanges a quick look with Devlin before answering. "Got caught up fixing that fence line on the north pasture. Lost track of time."

"Devlin," Jesse continues, his voice carrying that note of authority I remember from when we were younger. "Why don't you take care of the horses? I'll be along in a minute."

Devlin nods and leads both horses toward the barn without a word. The easy camaraderie between the brothers seems strained, like they're both carrying some invisible weight.

Jesse walks over to the porch, his boots making soft sounds on the worn wooden steps. In the pale moonlight, I can see the dust coating his clothes, the way his shirt sticks to his chest with sweat. But there's something else too—an edge to him that wasn't there this morning.

"Mind if I sit?" he asks, gesturing to the empty space beside me on the swing.

"Course not."

He settles next to me, and immediately the air fills with his scent—leather, horses, and something uniquely him that makes my pulse quicken. The swing creaks slightly under our combined weight, but it holds steady.

"So," I say, turning to study his profile. "Fixing fences in the dark? That's new."

Jesse chuckles, but it doesn't quite reach his eyes. "Not much choice when there's this much work to be done. Can't afford to lose cattle because of a broken fence."

He reaches into his shirt pocket and pulls out a pack of cigarettes, tapping one out. "You mind?"

I shake my head, watching as he lights it with practiced ease. The flame from his lighter briefly illuminates his face, highlighting the strong line of his jaw and the fullness of his lips. When he takes that first drag, I find myself staring at his mouth longer than I should.

"Want some?" He offers the cigarette to me.

I shouldn't. I quit smoking years ago when I moved to the city. But something about being back here, about sitting next to Jesse in the darkness, makes me want to reclaim pieces of who I used to be.

"Sure."

Our fingers brush as I take the cigarette from him, and the contact sends electricity up my arm. I take a slow drag, letting the familiar burn fill my lungs, then pass it back. We fall into an easy rhythm, sharing the cigarette while the swing moves gently back and forth.

"Remember when we used to sneak out here to smoke when we were teenagers?" Jesse asks, his voice softer now.

"You mean when you used to corrupt innocent little me?" I tease, bumping his shoulder with mine.

"Innocent." He laughs, and this time it sounds genuine. "You were never innocent, Aubree Weber. You were trouble from the day you learned to walk."

"Takes one to know one."

"True enough."

The silence that follows is comfortable, filled with shared memories and the gentle sounds of the night. Crickets chirp in the distance, and somewhere an owl calls out. This is the peace I missed in the city, the way the world slows down out here, the way you can actually hear yourself think.

"I missed this," I admit, surprised by my own honesty.

"What? Smoking?"

"No. Well, maybe a little." I smile. "I missed the quiet. The space to breathe. In Chicago, there was always noise, always something demanding your attention."

Jesse takes the cigarette back, his fingers lingering against mine longer than necessary. "What else did you miss?"

The question hangs in the air between us, loaded with implications I'm not sure I'm ready to explore. But the darkness makes me bold, and the nicotine has loosened my tongue.

"I missed you," I say quietly. "All of you, but...I missed you."

He goes very still beside me, the cigarette forgotten between his fingers. When he finally turns to look at me, his green eyes are intense in the moonlight.

"Aubree..."

"Don't." I shake my head. "Don't say whatever you're about to say. I know it's complicated. I know things are different now."

"Things have always been complicated between us."

"Have they?"

He considers this, taking another drag before answering. "Maybe not when we were kids. But we're not kids anymore."

"No, we're not."

The swing continues its gentle motion, but the air between us has changed, charged with an electricity that makes my skin tingle. I'm acutely aware of how close he is, how the moonlight plays across his features, how his breathing has changed to match mine.

"Aubree," he says again, his voice rougher now.

"Yeah?"

"There are things about me, about what I do...things you don't know."

I turn to face him fully, tucking one leg under me on the swing. "So tell me."

He's quiet for a long moment, clearly wrestling with something internal. Finally, he stubs out the cigarette on the porch railing and turns back to me.

"Some things are better left alone."

"Are they? Or are you just scared I won't like what I find?"

His laugh is bitter. "You definitely won't like what you find."

"Try me."

We're sitting closer now, close enough that I can see the flecks of gold in his green eyes, close enough to count the individual whiskers in his dark beard. My heart is pounding so hard I'm sure he can hear it.

"You always were too curious for your own good," he murmurs.

"And you always were too good at keeping secrets."

Something shifts in his expression, a darkness passing over his features like a cloud across the moon. "What makes you think I'm keeping secrets?"

"Because I know you, Jesse. I've known you my whole life." I reach out and touch his arm, feeling the solid muscle beneath his shirt. "And I know when you're lying."

His jaw tightens under my touch, but he doesn't pull away. "Maybe you don't know me as well as you think."

"Maybe I know you better than you know yourself."

The tension between us is almost unbearable now, thick as summer air before a storm. I can see the war playing out in his eyes, the struggle between whatever he's hiding and his desire to trust me.

"Aubree," he says, his voice barely above a whisper.

"What?"

"You need to let this go."

"Like hell I do." The words come out stronger than I intended. "I didn't let things go when we were kids, and I'm not about to start now."

Before I can react, his hand comes up to cup my face, his thumb tracing along my jawline. The touch is gentle but firm, and I can feel the calluses on his fingers from years of ranch work.

"You might not like what you find," he says, his voice rough with warning.

"I might surprise you."

For a moment, I think he's going to kiss me. His eyes drop to my lips, and I can feel the heat radiating from his body. But instead, he leans forward and presses his lips to my cheek, just below my ear. The kiss is soft but brief, over almost before it begins.

"Good night, Aubree," he whispers against my skin.

Then he's gone, standing up from the swing and walking away, leaving me sitting there with my heart racing and more questions than answers burning in my mind.

I touch my cheek where his lips were, still feeling the warmth of his kiss. Whatever Jesse is hiding, whatever secrets he and Devlin are keeping, I'm going to find out. He should know by now that telling me to let something go is the surest way to make me dig deeper.

Some things never change.

And right now, I'm grateful for that.

SIX
JESSE

"HOW'D THINGS GO LAST NIGHT?" Truett asks early the next morning, as we have coffee together at the barn.

The fucking sun hasn't even come up over the hills yet, and he wants me to get my thoughts together? Luckily for both of us, I'm used to it.

I take a drink, wincing. "Fuck, that's hot."

"But it's strong," Truett laughs.

Shaking my head, I set the cup down on the desk in his office. "Too fuckin' strong. Anyway, last night was successful. We picked up the package, and it's out in the east pasture."

"Did you have any problems?" he asks, leaning back in his chair. "I was worried since Aubree was here last night. We've gotten sloppier than we should since she's been gone."

Now, this puts me in a tough situation. Do I tell him that I spent most of the evening when I got back out with her behind the house? My cock gets slightly hard thinking about almost kissing her. In the end, I figure I should be honest. "She was on the swing last night when Devlin and I got back."

"Shit." He closes his eyes. "What did she say? What did you do?"

"Told her that we got caught up fixing the fence, and it got dark on us earlier than we'd anticipated. She seemed to buy it, and to keep the charade going, I sat out there with her for a while."

"It was midnight. She wasn't suspicious? That's the last thing I need. Her getting involved with what we've been doing to keep both places afloat since our parents died."

Don't I fuckin' know that. Not only that, but she'll be in as much danger as we are, day in and day out. The part of me that's always wanted to protect her is not happy with that, and won't stand for it. "Not that I could tell. We have to be honest and know that she might figure out what's going on, but we'll cross that bridge when we get to it."

"Sounds good. What does the rest of your day look like? Can I put you with Aubree?"

Fuck. My. Life. Does he realize he just keeps throwing his little sister at me? The part of me that's been obsessed with her since she was born? It answers the question. "Yeah, put her with me. I'll get as much done as I can before she comes out here in a few hours."

"Thank you." He claps me on the shoulder.

I drain the rest of my coffee, grimacing at the bitter burn, and head out to find Carson and Denver. The morning air is crisp, carrying the scent of hay and horses, along with something else. The lingering tension from last night's job. We can't afford to get sloppy, especially not now that Aubree's back.

I find my brothers near the equipment shed, Carson checking over some tools while Denver leans against the fence, smoking a cigarette. They both look up as I approach, and I can see the question in their eyes before either of them speaks.

"Truett happy with what went down last night?" Carson asks, setting down a wrench.

"Yup. He's more worried about Aubree figuring things out than he is about the actual job." I grab a fence post that's been leaning against the shed and test its weight. "Speaking of which, we need to talk about last night."

Denver flicks his cigarette butt into the dirt and crushes it under his boot heel. "Everything went smooth as silk. No complications, no witnesses, cattle are exactly where they need to be. It was an all-hands-on-deck situation, and us Nelson boys made sure things were taken care of."

"Good. But we need to stay sharp. With Aubree back, we can't have any more close calls like last night. She was outside when Devlin and I got back to the ranch. Luckily, I was able to play it off." I look between my brothers, making sure they understand the gravity of the situation. "She's smart, and she knows this ranch better than anyone. One slipup and she'll start asking questions we can't answer."

Carson nods, running a hand through his dark hair. "What's the timeline on moving the herd?"

"Denver's handling the brands and tags today," I say, turning to our youngest brother. "How long do you need?"

Denver straightens up, all business now. "Give me three days, maybe four. I want to make sure everything's perfect. The brands need to be clean, and the paperwork has to be airtight in case someone comes asking questions."

"Four days it is. After that, we move them to the holding pasture on the north side, then Carson takes them to market next week." I set the fence post back down and check my watch. "In the meantime, we keep doing regular ranch work, keep everything looking normal."

"What about Aubree?" Carson asks. "Truett's got you babysitting her today, right?"

The way he says it makes my jaw clench. "I'm not babysitting anyone. She's capable of handling ranch work."

Denver smirks. "That why you're wound up tighter than a tick on a hound dog this morning?"

"Fuck off, Denver." But there's no real heat in it. My brothers know me too well, know that Aubree has always been a weakness for me. "Just keep your heads down and do your jobs. We can't afford any mistakes."

"Speaking of mistakes," Carson says, his tone turning serious. "You sure sitting out on that swing with her last night was a good idea? Getting close to her while we're in the middle of all this?"

The question hits harder than I'd like to admit. Am I making a mistake? Probably. But the memory of her sitting there in the moonlight, looking lost and vulnerable, makes my chest tight. "It was nice talking to her, and it wasn't like I was going to leave her out there alone."

"Just be careful," Denver says, and for once, there's no teasing in his voice. "We all care about Aubree, but if she finds out what we're doing..."

"She won't." The words come out sharper than I intended. "I'll make sure of it."

We spend the next hour going over the details—which

pastures to avoid, how to explain any unusual activity, what story to stick to if anyone asks questions. By the time we're done, the sun is fully up, painting the sky in shades of orange and pink that remind me of Aubree's cheeks when she blushes.

Christ, I need to get my head straight.

I'm just finishing up some paperwork when I see her walking toward the barn, and my mouth goes dry. She's wearing jeans that hug her curves in all the right places and a simple T-shirt that somehow makes her look both innocent and sinful at the same time. Her honey-blonde hair catches the morning light, and those deep brown eyes are focused on me with an intensity that makes my pulse quicken.

"Morning, Jesse," she says, and there's something shy in her voice that wasn't there yesterday.

"Morning, Bree." I clear my throat, trying to ignore the way my name sounds when she says it. "Ready to get your hands dirty?"

She tilts her head, studying me with those intelligent eyes. "Depends on what kind of dirty we're talking about."

The innocent question hits me like a punch to the gut, sending heat straight to my groin. Does she have any idea what she does to me? "Ranch work," I manage to say, my voice coming out rougher than intended. "Cleaning stalls, checking fences, the usual."

"Sounds perfect." She falls into step beside me as we head toward the barn. "I've missed this place more than I realized."

"It's missed you too." The words slip out before I can stop them, and I see her glance up at me with surprise.

We work in comfortable silence for a while, me showing her which stalls need attention, her falling back into the rhythm of ranch work like she never left. But I'm hyperaware of every movement she makes, every soft grunt of effort, every time she pushes her hair back from her face.

This is going to be a long day.

As we head back toward the house for lunch, I catch sight of Denver near the east pasture, right where our "package" is grazing. He's got his tools with him, ready to start the delicate work of branding and tagging. The sight reminds me of exactly how complicated my life has become, keeping secrets from the woman I can't stop thinking about, while trying to save the ranch that means everything to all of us.

"Jesse?" Aubree's voice pulls me back to the present.

"Yeah?"

"Thanks for last night. And for today. I know I'm probably not much help yet, getting back into the swing of things."

I stop walking and turn to face her, taking in the genuine gratitude in her expression. "Bree, you're always welcome here. This is your home."

She smiles, and it's like the sun coming out from behind clouds. "I'm starting to remember that."

As we continue toward the house, I make a silent promise to myself. Whatever it takes, I'll keep her safe. Even if it means keeping secrets that could destroy everything between us.

SEVEN
AUBREE

I WORRIED that I wouldn't sleep well out here, without the sounds of the city around me. Worried that it would be too quiet, or I would be thinking too much about everything I left behind. Surprisingly, none of that bothered me, and I slept better than I have in the past two months.

Heading downstairs, I smell coffee, and I know it's not from Truett. Taking the steps quickly, I rush around the corner, and smile when I see the older gentleman I always thought of as my grandfather figure. "Cookie!"

"Hey, girlie! Welcome home." He rushes forward, opening his arms up for me.

I wrap him up in a hug and then pull back, looking up at the big, burly man. The years since I've been gone show in the deeper wrinkles on his face and the snow-white tint of his hair, but those kind brown eyes are still the same. "Thank you. I missed you."

"Missed you too. Coffee? What do you want for breakfast? I figure being a big-city girl, your tastes may have changed."

He's right. A lot about me has changed, but there's one breakfast that always makes my mouth water. "Same as always, Cook. Egg sandwich, tomatoes, hash browns, and coffee as black as my soul."

He throws his head back, laughing. As he smiles over at me, for the first time, I feel like everything is going to be okay.

Cookie bustles around the kitchen with the same energy he's always had, cracking eggs with practiced precision and sliding bread into the ancient toaster that's been on this counter since I was ten years old. The familiar sounds and smells wrap around me like a warm blanket, erasing the years and heartbreak that brought me back here.

"So," he says, settling across from me with his own cup of coffee. "How's it feel to be back?"

"Different than I expected." I take a sip of the strong black coffee and sigh contentedly. "Good different, though. I forgot how peaceful it is here."

"Peaceful's one word for it," Cookie chuckles. "Though I'd say it's been anything but peaceful around here lately. Your brothers have been working themselves to the bone trying to keep both ranches running."

A pang of guilt hits me. While I was off in the city, pursuing my own dreams and dealing with my own disasters, Truett was here carrying the weight of everything our parents left behind. "I should have come back sooner."

"Nonsense." Cookie waves a dismissive hand. "You needed to spread your wings, see what else was out there. Can't fault a person for that. Besides, you're here now when they need you most."

The eggs sizzle in the pan, and Cookie flips them with a practiced flick of his wrist. "Speaking of which, how'd your evening go last night? I saw you and Jesse out on the swing."

Heat creeps up my neck at the memory. That brief kiss has been replaying in my mind since the moment it happened. "It was...nice. We just talked."

Cookie gives me a knowing look but doesn't push. He's always been good at reading between the lines, understanding what people don't say as much as what they do. "Jesse's a good man. Loyal as they come. Been like family to us since your parents took him in."

"I know." The words come out softer than I intended. Jesse has always been part of the landscape of this place, as permanent and solid as the mountains on the horizon. But last night, something shifted. The way he looked at me, touched me—it wasn't the same protective, brotherly affection I remembered from my teenage years.

Cookie slides my breakfast across the table, the egg sandwich perfectly constructed with thick slices of fresh tomato, and the hash browns golden and crispy just the way I like them. "Eat up. Spring's been mild so far, but we're expecting a cold snap this weekend. Need to make sure you've got your strength up for whatever work Truett has planned for you."

We talk about inconsequential things while I eat, the early wildflowers starting to bloom in the pastures, Cookie's ongoing battle with the ranch's ancient plumbing. It's comfortable, familiar conversation that doesn't require me to think about complicated things like failed relationships or uncertain futures or the way Jesse's green eyes seemed to see straight through me last night.

"This is exactly what I needed," I tell Cookie as I finish the last bite of my sandwich.

"What's that?"

"This. Normal. Just sitting here talking about whether the old water heater is going to make it through another winter."

Cookie reaches over and pats my hand. "Sometimes normal is the most healing thing there is."

Just as I'm draining the last of my coffee, Truett walks through the kitchen door, his hair still damp from a shower and his work shirt clean but already wrinkled from the morning's activities.

"Morning, sis. Sleep okay?"

"Better than I have in months." I stand up and carry my dishes to the sink, rinsing them out of habit more than necessity. Cookie always insists on doing the cleaning himself.

"Good. I've got you paired up with Jesse again today. Just until you get back into the swing of things."

My stomach does a little flip at the mention of Jesse's name, and I hope it doesn't show on my face. "Sounds good."

But Truett is already studying me with that big brother intuition that used to drive me crazy as a teenager. "Everything okay? You look a little flushed."

"Just the coffee," I lie, waving toward Cookie. "He still makes it strong enough to wake the dead."

"That's the only way to make coffee," Cookie declares from where he's already started washing my dishes, despite my protests.

Truett grins. "Well, Jesse's probably waiting for you by now. He likes to get an early start."

"I'll head out there now." I give Cookie another quick hug. "Thanks for breakfast."

"Anytime, girlie. You just holler if you need anything."

The morning air is crisp and clean, carrying the scent of hay and horses and the oncoming spring. The scent of grass hangs in the air, along with the dirt that's always around. I'm halfway to the barn when I see Jesse walking toward me, and my breath catches in my throat.

How did I not notice yesterday how absolutely devastating he looks? He's always been handsome, tall, and lean, with those striking green eyes and that dark beard that frames his full mouth perfectly. But there's something different about him now, something more mature and confident that makes my pulse quicken.

His jeans hug his long legs, and his work shirt is rolled up to reveal tattooed forearms that flex as he adjusts his hat. When he sees me, those green eyes lock onto mine with an intensity that makes me feel like he can see every thought I've ever had.

"Morning, Bree."

"Morning." My voice comes out breathier than I intended, and I clear my throat. "Ready to put me to work?"

Something flashes in his eyes. Amusement maybe, or something darker. "Always ready to work with you."

The way he says it makes heat pool low in my belly, and I have to look away before I do something embarrassing like stare at his mouth and remember how it felt against my cheek last night.

He leads me into the barn, explaining which stalls need

mucking out and where to find the tools. It's work I've done a thousand times before, work I did just yesterday, but I let him explain anyway, partly because I'm out of practice and partly because I like listening to his voice, deep and rough with that slight drawl that makes even mundane instructions sound sexy.

"I'll start on this end," I say, grabbing a pitchfork. "Work my way down."

"Sounds good. I'll be right across the aisle if you need anything."

We fall into a comfortable rhythm, the familiar work coming back to me quickly. The physical labor feels good after years of sitting behind a desk, and I lose myself in the simple satisfaction of making tangible progress. Clean stall, fresh bedding, move on to the next one.

I'm bent over, spreading fresh straw in the third stall, when I feel eyes on me. Glancing over my shoulder, I catch Jesse watching me with an expression that makes my skin tingle.

"I can feel you lookin' at my ass," I say, straightening up and turning to face him with a teasing smile.

His eyes darken, and he leans against his pitchfork with predatory grace. "Negative, Bree. I'd like to spank the hell out of it."

The words hit me like a physical blow, sending heat racing through my veins and making my knees weak. The frank hunger in his voice, the way he's looking at me like he wants to devour me–it's nothing like the gentle, almost hesitant man who kissed me so softly last night.

"Jesse..." I breathe, not sure if it's a warning or an invitation.

He straightens up, his jaw clenching like he's fighting some internal battle. "Sorry. That was...inappropriate."

"Was it?" I take a step closer to him, emboldened by the obvious effect I'm having on him. "Because I don't think I minded."

For a moment, the air between us crackles with tension so thick I can almost taste it. His green eyes search my face, and I can see the war between desire and restraint playing out in his expression.

Then, he takes a step back, putting distance between us. "We should get back to work."

Part of me wants to push, to close the distance he just created and see what happens. But the rational part of my brain knows he's right. I'm fresh off a devastating breakup, he works for my brother, and I'm in no position to make smart decisions about anything, let alone gorgeous cowboys who look at me like they want to consume me whole.

So I go back to mucking stalls, hyperaware of every movement he makes, every breath he takes. The work that felt meditative before now feels charged with electricity, every accidental brush of our hands when we pass each other sending sparks up my arm.

By lunchtime, I'm wound tighter than a spring and trying very hard not to think about exactly what Jesse might do if he decided to act on his threat about spanking me.

We break for sandwiches that Cookie packed for us, sitting on hay bales in the shade of the barn. The conversation stays safely on neutral topics—the weather, the cattle, plans for the upcoming week. But underneath the mundane words, I can feel a current of awareness humming between us.

"How long are you planning to stay?" Jesse asks as we finish eating.

"I don't know yet." It's an honest answer. "As long as I'm needed, I guess. As long as I can be useful."

"You're always useful here, Bree. This is your home."

There's something in his voice. A warmth and certainty that makes my chest tight with emotion I'm not ready to examine too closely.

The afternoon passes in much the same way, working side by side, stealing glances when we think the other isn't looking, the tension between us building with every passing hour. By the time the sun starts sinking toward the horizon, painting the sky in shades of gold and pink, I'm exhausted from more than just physical labor.

"We should head up to the house," Jesse says, checking his watch. "Cookie said dinner would be ready around six, and the other boys will be coming up to eat."

"The other boys?"

"Denver and Austin. They don't usually eat with the family, but Cookie insists when there's company." He gives me a small smile. "Apparently, you count as special company today."

I laugh, turning to face him. "Cookie just needs an excuse to bring everybody together." My phone vibrates. I pull it out of my back pocket, a smile working its way across my face as I see a text from Nora.

> **N**
> Girls' night moved up. Meet me at the Rusty Spur?

Why the hell not?

A
I'll be there!

As we walk toward the house, our hands brush accidentally, and I feel that same electric jolt I've been fighting all day. Jesse's step falters slightly, and when I look up at him, his jaw is clenched tight.

This is going to be a long dinner.

EIGHT
JESSE

MY EYES FOLLOW Aubree as she heads up the stairs to her room so she can change into some cleaner clothes. The worn jeans cup her ass cheeks as she moves, and I have to shake my head to clear the thoughts.

Denver and Austin come crashing through the front door, Carson not far behind. "Y'all go clean up before we have a seat." My voice is harsher than I mean for it to be. "We've got a woman here now."

All of them look at me with their eyebrows raised, like they know something I don't, but I glare right back at them. It's a battle of wills as we face off, but it's always been me against these three, unless someone's giving the shit, then it's us against the world.

"Hell..." Carson sighs before turning on his heel and heading toward the downstairs bathroom. The other two follow.

Happy that they did as I asked, I head into the kitchen to

wash up, bumping into Cookie. "Whoa..." I reach out, steadying him.

"Shewwww, that was almost the plate of steak." He holds up a platter, showing me what he was talking about. "Thanks for saving it."

"It was almost my fault it got lost." My boots scuff against the hardwood as I walk over to the sink, a laugh in my voice. "There'd be a revolt, and I'm not sure I could handle that today." Not after having to be as close as I was to Aubree and not lose my mind in the process.

Truett comes down the stairs. He glances up at me. "I've gotta go do some business tonight. Aubree mentioned she and Nora would be heading to the Rusty Spur tonight. Any chance you can go and make sure they don't get into trouble?"

Wonder when she found out she was doing that? She hasn't mentioned it to me all day, and it wasn't at all what I was expecting, but it's something I can do without much issue. "Yeah, I'll drive, and I'll sit there like a fucking mafia boss, daring others to step up to them. Sound good?"

He laughs, rolling the sleeves of his shirt up. "Exactly what I was thinking of."

"Truett, I don't need a babysitter," Aubree complains, making an apppearance.

She's completely refreshed and gorgeous in a clean pair of jeans and a long-sleeved shirt that hugs her curves.

"That may be true, but the cowboys in this town need one."

Her mouth curls up, and she flips him the finger. "Fine."

The tension in the room shifts as we all gather around the dining table. Cookie's outdone himself tonight, with thick steaks, loaded baked potatoes, and green beans that actually taste like something other than mush. The kind of meal that should have us all talking and laughing, but instead, I find myself sitting back, watching.

And what I'm watching is making my blood simmer.

Denver's telling some story about a bull that nearly took his head off last week, but his eyes keep drifting to Aubree. The way she laughs, throwing her head back, exposing that elegant line of her throat. The bastard's eating it up.

"You should've seen this thing," Denver continues, gesturing wildly with his fork. "Fifteen hundred pounds of pure attitude, and prettier than most women I know." He shoots Aubree a look. "Present company excluded, of course."

She grins, and I want to punch him. "Of course. I'd hate to think I was losing to a bull in the looks department."

Austin jumps in, not to be outdone. "Speaking of pretty, that shirt's a good color on you, Aubree. Brings out your eyes."

My grip tightens on my knife until my knuckles go white. These assholes are flirting with her right in front of me, and she's flirting right back. The easy way she smiles at them, how she leans forward when they talk, the little touches she gives their arms when they make her laugh–it's all innocent enough, but it's driving me fucking crazy.

Carson, never one to be left out, decides to join the Aubree appreciation society. "Remember that time you convinced us to go skinny dipping in the creek when we were teenagers? You were always the brave one."

"I was also the stupid one," she laughs, and the sound goes straight through me. "Truett nearly killed me when he found out."

"Worth it though," Carson says with a wink that makes me want to throw my steak knife at his head.

I cut into my meat with more force than necessary, the sound of the knife hitting the plate sharp enough to make everyone glance my way. But I don't say anything. I just chew and watch and let the anger build in my chest like a storm gathering strength.

Truett, oblivious to the undercurrents swirling around his dining table, is busy planning out tomorrow's work. "We need to move the cattle from the south pasture before this weather hits. Austin, I want you and Carson on the four-wheelers, pushing them north. Denver, you and Jesse can take the horses and work the stragglers."

"Sounds good, boss," Denver says, but his attention is still on Aubree. "Maybe Aubree can come help. She always was better on a horse than half of us."

The suggestion hits me like a physical blow. The thought of spending hours in the saddle with her, working side by side, her body moving in rhythm with her horse...I push the image away before it can take root.

"I don't think that's necessary," I say, my voice coming out rougher than I intended.

All eyes turn to me, and I realize I've just revealed more than I meant to. Aubree's looking at me with those deep brown eyes, a question forming on her lips that I don't want to answer.

"Jesse's right," Truett says, missing the tension entirely. "You haven't been on a horse in a long time. We shouldn't throw you back in the thick of things too fast."

The conversation moves on, but I can feel Aubree's gaze lingering on me. She knows something's off, but she can't put her finger on what. Good. The last thing I need is for her to figure out that watching my brothers flirt with her is making me lose my goddamn mind.

As the meal continues, I become a student of details I wish I could ignore. The way she cuts her steak into precise little pieces before eating them. How she always takes a sip of water after every few bites. The unconscious way she tucks her honey-blonde hair behind her ear when she's listening to someone talk.

And the worst part? She's completely unaware of the effect she's having, not just on my brothers, but on me. Every laugh, every smile, every casual touch is like a match struck against my already frayed nerves.

"Remember that time we all went to the county fair?" Austin's saying now, and I know exactly where this story is heading. "And Aubree entered the pie-eating contest?"

"Oh god," she groans, covering her face with her hands. "Don't."

"She was so determined to beat old Mrs. Henderson," Austin continues, grinning. "Ended up with blueberry pie from her hairline to her chin."

"And you looked beautiful doing it," Denver adds with a grin that makes me want to put him through the wall.

Carson nods sagely. "Most attractive pie-eating contest contestant in county fair history."

She's laughing now, that full-bodied laugh that does things to my insides I don't want to think about. "You're all ridiculous."

"Ridiculously right," Austin says, and there's something in his tone that makes my jaw clench.

I've had enough.

Standing abruptly, I push my chair back from the table. "I'm gonna go check on the horses."

"Jesse," Aubree starts, but I'm already moving.

"Finish eating," I tell her without looking back. "We'll head out in twenty."

The cool evening air hits my face as I step onto the porch, but it does nothing to cool the fire burning in my chest. I need to get my head on straight before I do something stupid, like punch one of my brothers or pin Aubree against the nearest wall and show her exactly what I think about her flirting with them.

The horses are fine, of course. They're always fine. But I spend the next fifteen minutes in the barn anyway, breathing in the familiar smells of hay and leather, trying to talk myself down from the ledge I'm standing on.

This is Aubree. Truett's little sister. The girl I've known since she was in pigtails and braces. The woman I've spent the last ten years trying not to think about in any way that wasn't completely platonic.

But watching her tonight, seeing the way she's grown into herself, confident and beautiful and completely unaware of her own power...it's breaking down every wall I've built to keep these feelings locked away.

And the worst part? I think she knows exactly what she's doing to me.

When I finally head back to the house, everyone's finishing up dessert. Cookie's made his famous apple pie, and there's easy laughter flowing around the table. For a moment, I almost wish I could join in, be part of the easy camaraderie instead of standing on the outside, watching and wanting what I can't have.

"There he is," Truett says as I walk back in. "Everything good with the horses?"

"Everything's fine." I lean against the doorframe, studying the scene. Aubree's got a small smile playing at the corners of her mouth, like she's got a secret she's not sharing.

"Well, if you two are heading to the Rusty Spur, you better get going," Truett says, checking his watch. "Gets crowded after nine, and you'll never find a parking spot."

Aubree stands, brushing invisible crumbs from her jeans. "Let me grab my jacket."

"Meet me at the truck," I tell her, my voice coming out more commanding than I intended.

She pauses, looking at me with those brown eyes that see too much. For a second, I think she's going to call me on my tone, but then she just nods.

"See you boys later," she says to my brothers, giving them each a quick hug that makes my teeth grind together.

As she heads upstairs, I catch Denver watching her go with a look I don't like. "Something to say?" I ask him.

He shrugs, but there's a knowing glint in his eye. "Just wondering when you're gonna stop pretending you don't want her."

Before I can respond, he's walking away, leaving me standing there with my hands clenched into fists and the truth sitting heavy in my chest.

I do want her. God help me, I want her more than I've ever wanted anything in my life. And tonight, sitting in a crowded bar, watching other men look at her the way I've been trying not to...it's going to be the longest night of my life.

NINE
AUBREE

"LOOK AT YOU." I grin as I approach Jesse's truck.

He's standing there, waiting for me. His back rests against the passenger door of his truck, and those green eyes are tracking me as my boots crunch on the gravel driveway. "Look at me, what?"

"Out here waiting for me. You gonna be all gentlemanly and open my door?" I tease, my tongue coming out to swipe at my dry bottom lip.

"Yeah," he reaches forward, rubbing the moisture off. "Now get your ass up in this truck before I show you what I'd like to do to those ruby red lips."

The heat in his gaze is enough to ignite a fire between the two of us. I know I'm playing with this flame, and I might get burned, but I can't think of a better way to go. Grabbing hold of the door handle, I yank it open and go to hitch my foot on the running board, but a warm hand around my hip stops my forward motion.

I'm tugged back to Jesse. "Don't make me fight some asshole guys at this bar who watched *Yellowstone* and decided they wanted to ride a horse."

I close my eyes when I feel the palm of his hand caressing my ass. "Don't give me ideas, Jesse Nelson. I'm just going to have fun with my friends. My brother asked you to be my bodyguard." Without another word, I take the passenger seat and then reach out to close the door.

He moves back with a smirk on his face. "We're gonna end up acting on this, Bree."

"What's that?"

"The unfinished business we have between us. You kissed me once, and I didn't respond the way I should've. You do it again? I'm not letting the moment stop me. Truett and our relationship be damned." He doesn't say anything else. He just closes the door and walks around the front of the truck before getting in on his side.

The air in the cab feels thick and charged as Jesse starts the engine. The rumble of the diesel fills the silence between us, but it doesn't mask the tension that's been building all evening. I can feel it crackling like electricity, dangerous and irresistible.

I steal a glance at his profile as he backs out of the driveway. The dashboard lights cast shadows across his strong jaw, highlighting the dark scruff that covers it. His hands on the steering wheel are large and calloused from years of ranch work, and I find myself remembering how one of them felt against my hip just moments ago.

"You're staring," he says without taking his eyes off the road, but there's amusement in his voice.

"Maybe." I don't deny it. There's no point. "You were pretty quiet at dinner."

His jaw tics. "Had nothing to say."

That's a lie, and we both know it. I saw the way he was watching me, the way his grip on his knife kept tightening every time one of his brothers made me laugh. Jesse Nelson has plenty to say. He's just not saying it.

"Right." I turn in my seat to face him better. "Nothing at all to say about Denver calling me prettier than most women he knows? Or Austin complimenting my shirt? Or Carson bringing up skinny dipping?"

His knuckles go white on the steering wheel. "They're flirting with you."

"And that bothers you because...?"

He shoots me a look that's all heat and frustration. "You know why."

I do know why. But I want to hear him say it. I want him to admit what's been simmering between us for years, what nearly boiled over that night I kissed him and he pulled away like I'd burned him.

Instead of pushing, I settle back in my seat and watch the familiar landscape roll by. We pass the old Miller farm, the abandoned gas station that's been closed for as long as I can remember, and the creek where we used to swim as kids. Everything looks different in the darkness, but the memories are just as vivid.

"Remember when we used to sneak out here on Friday nights?" I ask, my voice softer now.

His expression gentles slightly. "You mean when you used to sneak out and drag us along with you?"

"I never had to drag you anywhere, Jesse Nelson. You were always right there, ready for whatever trouble I was cooking up."

"Someone had to keep you from getting yourself killed."

"Is that what you were doing?" I study his profile again, noting the way his mouth curves slightly. "Keeping me safe?"

"Always."

The simple word hits me harder than it should. There's something in the way he says it, like it's not just about the past. Like it's a promise that extends to right now, to the future, to whatever comes next.

We fall silent again, but it's a different kind of quiet now. Less charged, more...expectant. Like we're both waiting for something to happen, something that's been building for years.

The Rusty Spur comes into view, its neon sign flickering against the night sky. The parking lot is already crowded with trucks and SUVs, and I can hear the faint sound of music drifting from inside.

Jesse finds a parking spot near the back, away from the main crowd. He kills the engine but doesn't make any move to get out. Instead, he turns to face me, those green eyes serious.

"I meant what I said earlier, Bree. About the unfinished business between us."

My heart starts beating faster. "I know you did."

"And I meant what I said about not letting the moment stop me next time."

"Good." The word comes out breathier than I intended. "Because I'm tired of pretending too."

Something flashes in his eyes. Surprise, maybe? Or relief, like he wasn't expecting me to be so direct about it.

Before either of us can say anything else, my phone buzzes

with a text. Nora, wondering where I am. The spell is broken, and Jesse's pulling his keys from the ignition.

"Come on," he says, his voice rougher than usual. "Let's go before I do something that'll get us both in trouble."

The Rusty Spur is exactly what you'd expect from a small-town bar. Dim lighting, peanut shells on the floor, and a mechanical bull that nobody's brave enough to ride after eight o'clock. The crowd is a mix of ranchers, college kids from the community college, and tourists who wandered off the beaten path.

I spot Nora immediately. She's claimed a table near the back, away from the main dance floor, but with a perfect view of everything happening. Her dark hair is pulled back in a messy bun, and she's wearing the kind of outfit that says she's trying to look casual but still wants to turn heads.

"There you are!" she calls out as I approach, but her eyes immediately shift to Jesse, who's hovering behind me like a gorgeous, brooding shadow. "And you brought a chaperone."

"Truett's orders," I explain, sliding into the chair across from her. "Jesse's supposed to make sure I don't get into trouble."

"Right." Nora's grin is wicked. "Just trouble, huh?"

I feel heat creep up my neck. Nora's been my best friend since high school, which means she knows exactly what kind of trouble Jesse Nelson represents. She also knows about the kiss, about the years of unresolved tension, about the way I've never quite gotten over the boy who grew up next door.

Jesse doesn't sit down. Instead, he nods toward the bar. "I'll be over there. Holler if you need anything."

"Such a gentleman," Nora says once he's out of earshot, but her tone is teasing. "And by gentleman, I mean he looks like he wants to murder every man in this place who so much as glances your way."

I watch as Jesse claims a spot at the bar where he has a clear view of our table. He orders what I know will be a beer he'll nurse all night and settles in to watch. Even from across the room, I can feel the weight of his attention.

"So," Nora says, pulling my focus back to her. "How's it going with the whole living-in-the-same-house-as-the-man-you've-been-in-love-with-since-forever thing?"

The other girls at the table—Lennon, Atlee, and Emerson—all snicker. We'd all been friends in high school, except for Atlee, who's Lennon's little sister. And while I'd kept up with Nora, the other ones I didn't check in with like I should've.

"It's..." I struggle for the right words. "Complicated."

"Everything about the Nelson family is complicated," Atlee says, lifting her beer in salute. "Wish I could get Devlin to look at me the way he's looking at you."

The group snickers as Nora comments, "The best kind of love stories usually are complicated." She signals the waitress and orders us both drinks. "Tell us everything."

So I do. I tell them about the tension at dinner, about the way Jesse's been watching me, about the conversation in the truck.

"Damn, girl," Nora breathes when I finish. "That man has it bad."

"You think?"

"Honey, I think if any of those cowboys over there even think about approaching this table, your bodyguard is going to end up in jail for assault." She glances toward the bar, where

Jesse is still watching us with predatory focus. "The question is, what are you gonna do about it?"

Before I can answer, the energy in the bar shifts. There's a buzz of excitement near the door, and I turn to see what's caused it.

Truett.

My brother cuts an imposing figure as he scans the room, his business apparently finished earlier than expected. He's still in his work clothes—dark jeans and a button-down shirt that shows off the physique that comes from a lifetime of physical labor.

But I'm not watching Truett. I'm watching Nora.

The expression on her face is one I've seen a thousand times over the years, but she always thinks she's hiding it. The way her eyes soften, the slight parting of her lips, the unconscious way she straightens her shoulders—it's the look of a woman seeing the man she's been in love with for most of her adult life.

"Earth to Nora," I say softly.

She blinks and turns back to me, a flush creeping up her neck. "What?"

"You're staring."

"No, I'm not."

"Right. And I suppose your face always turns that particular shade of pink when you're not staring at my brother."

She groans and drops her head into her hands. "Is it that obvious?"

"Only to someone who's known you for fifteen years." I lean forward, lowering my voice. "When are you going to tell him?"

"Tell him what? That I've been harboring a pathetic crush on him for the last ten years? That I've turned down three marriage proposals because none of them were him? That I lie awake at night wondering what it would be like if he looked at me the way he looks at his precious ranch?"

Her voice cracks on the last words, and my heart breaks a little for my best friend. I've watched her love my brother from a distance for years, always hoping he'd finally see what was right in front of him.

"It's not pathetic," I tell her firmly. "And maybe it's time to take a chance. What's the worst that could happen?"

"He could say no. Things could get weird. I could lose the best friendship I've ever had." She lifts her head, and there are tears threatening at the corners of her eyes. "I could lose him completely."

"Or," I counter gently. "You could gain everything you've ever wanted."

Before she can respond, Truett appears at our table. Up close, I can see he's showered and changed since dinner. His hair is still damp, and he smells like the expensive cologne he only wears when he's trying to impress someone.

"Ladies," he says with that easy smile that's broken hearts from here to Austin. "Mind if I join you?"

"Of course not," I say, shooting Nora a meaningful look. "We were just talking about taking chances."

Truett slides into the chair next to Nora, and I watch as she goes perfectly still. He's close enough that their arms are almost touching, close enough that she could lean into him if she had the courage.

"Speaking of taking chances," Truett says, his attention focused entirely on Nora. "Would you like to dance?"

The question hangs in the air between them, loaded with

possibilities. Nora's eyes go wide, and for a moment I think she might actually faint.

"I...what?"

"Dance," Truett repeats, standing and extending his hand. "With me. Unless you've got two left feet since the last time we tried this."

I hold my breath, watching as Nora stares at his outstretched hand like it might bite her. This is it, her chance to take that leap she's been too scared to take for ten years.

Finally, slowly, she places her hand in his. "I'd like that."

They head toward the small dance floor, where a few other couples are swaying to the slow song the band is playing. I watch as Truett pulls her close, one hand settling on her waist, the other still holding hers. Even from across the room, I can see the moment something shifts between them. The way Nora's face tilts up toward his, the way his thumb traces gentle circles on her waist, the way they move together like they've been doing this for years instead of minutes.

"Looks like your friend's finally getting her shot."

I turn to find Jesse standing beside our table, two fresh drinks in his hands. He sets one in front of me before taking Nora's abandoned chair.

"About time," I agree, accepting the drink gratefully. "I was starting to think they'd both die of old age before one of them made a move."

"Sometimes the best things are worth waiting for."

There's something in his tone that makes me look at him more carefully. He's watching Truett and Nora on the dance floor, but I get the feeling he's talking about more than just their relationship.

"Is that what you've been doing, Jesse? Waiting?"

He turns those green eyes on me, and the intensity in them takes my breath away. "Maybe. Question is, are you done waiting too?"

The music shifts to something faster, but Truett and Nora don't seem to notice. They're lost in their own little world, finally allowing themselves to feel what they've been fighting for years.

"Dance with me," I say suddenly, standing before I can lose my nerve.

Jesse looks surprised. "Bree..."

"You heard what you told me in the truck. About not letting the moment stop you next time." I hold out my hand, mirroring what Truett did with Nora. "Well, this is a moment, Jesse Nelson. What are you gonna do about it?"

TEN
JESSE

WHAT ARE *you gonna do about it?* I repeat the question in my head, trying to figure out if this is some sort of trick or if Aubree is really testing me.

It's crazy. With the shit we've got going on behind the scenes at the ranch, and her coming back? This should be the last thing on my mind, but I go back to the twenty-something-year-old I was when she kissed me.

I didn't realize what that meant, or what kind of gift she was giving me. To be honest, I still can't let myself think that far ahead, not when we're courting danger every couple of weeks. But tonight? I just wanna be a regular guy with the woman he hasn't been able to get out of his mind for years.

Reaching out, I grab her hand, pulling her up and closer to me. "Let's go."

My voice is barely loud enough to be heard, but hear it she does. Wrapping her arms around my neck, she scoots in so that our bodies are touching. I link my arms around her waist as

"Something in the Orange" starts playing from the jukebox in the corner.

She closes her eyes and leans her head against my shoulder.

The lyrics hit hard, about when your woman tucks her head between your collar and jaw. That's right where she is right now, and if I could keep her here forever, I would. There's an overwhelming urge for me to tell her what's been happening.

"Bree..." I start.

"Jesse," she whispers. "Don't. Don't tell me we shouldn't be doing this, that it's going to end before it even gets started. That it'll end badly. Give me these few moments. Can you do that for me?"

The desperation in her voice cuts right through me. Whatever brought her back here, whatever she's running from, it's eating at her just as much as our secrets are eating at me. Maybe we both deserve this moment of peace, this illusion that we're just two people who care about each other without all the complications.

"Yeah," I murmur against her hair, breathing in the familiar scent that's haunted my dreams for years. "I can give you that."

My arms tighten around her waist, pulling her impossibly closer. The heat of her body against mine sends electricity shooting through my veins. She fits against me like she was made for this spot, like all the years apart were just a mistake that's finally being corrected.

The song fades out, and another one begins, something slow and mournful that speaks of longing and second chances. We continue swaying, moving together like we've been dancing for years instead of minutes. Her fingers play with the hair at the nape of my neck, sending shivers down my spine.

"Are you happy to be home?" I ask, my lips brushing against her temple.

She's quiet for so long, I wonder if she heard me. When she finally speaks, her voice is barely audible over the music. "I'm happy to be home, but not happy about what brought me here."

The words hit me like a punch to the gut. I knew there had to be something. Aubree never would have come back willingly. She was too proud, too determined to make it on her own in the big city. Whatever happened must have been bad enough to drive her back to a place she'd sworn she'd never return to.

"What brought you back, Bree?" I pull back slightly so I can see her face, but she keeps her eyes closed.

I feel her body tense against mine, her fingers stilling in my hair. For a moment, I think she might actually tell me. Then she opens those deep brown eyes and gives me a smile that doesn't quite reach them.

"You're gonna have to work a lot harder than that to get me to spill all my secrets, Jesse Nelson."

The challenge in her voice makes something primal stir in my chest. I've always loved her fire, the way she never makes anything easy. Even when we were kids, she'd make me work for every smile, every laugh, every moment of her attention.

"Is that so?" I drawl, letting my hands drift lower to rest at the small of her back.

"Mm-hmm." She leans into me again, but this time there's a different energy between us. Less desperate, more playful. "I'm not the same girl who left here, you know."

"I can see that." And I can. There's a hardness to her now that wasn't there before, a wariness in her eyes that speaks of experiences I can only imagine. But underneath it all, she's still the Aubree who used to steal my breath with just a look.

We dance through two more songs, lost in our own little world. The bar could burn down around us, and I wouldn't notice. All that exists is the feel of her in my arms, the soft sound of her breathing, the way she melts against me like she belongs there.

But eventually, the music stops and the harsh overhead lights flicker on. Last call echoes through the room, shattering the spell we've been under. Reality comes crashing back—the ranch, the secrets, all the reasons why this is complicated.

"Guess that's our cue," Aubree says softly, but she doesn't immediately pull away.

"Guess so." I reluctantly loosen my hold on her, already missing the contact. "Come on. I'll drive you home."

The ride back to the ranch is quiet, filled with a tension that has nothing to do with awkwardness and everything to do with the electricity still crackling between us. Every time I glance over at her, she's looking out the window, but I can feel her awareness of me like a living thing.

When I pull up in front of the main house, neither of us moves to get out. The silence stretches between us, heavy with all the things we're not saying.

"Thank you," she finally says, turning to face me. "For tonight. For giving me those moments."

"Anytime." The words come out rougher than I intended, weighted with promises I'm not sure I should be making.

She reaches for the door handle, but I catch her wrist, stopping her. "Bree."

She turns back to me, and before I can second-guess myself,

I'm leaning across the space between us. My hand cups her cheek, thumb tracing across her soft skin, and then my lips are on hers.

The kiss starts gentle, tentative, like I'm afraid she might bolt. But then she sighs into my mouth and her hand fists in my shirt, pulling me closer. The taste of her explodes across my tongue, whiskey and something uniquely Aubree that I've never been able to forget.

When we finally break apart, we're both breathing hard. Her lips are swollen, her eyes dark with desire, and it takes every ounce of self-control I possess not to drag her back to me.

"That's not all I'm gonna steal," I tell her, my voice hoarse with want. "Before this is over, I'm gonna have your heart too."

The boldness of the statement surprises even me, but I don't take it back. I can't. After tonight, after feeling her in my arms again, I know I'm not walking away a second time.

A slow grin spreads across her face, transforming her from beautiful to devastating. "I can't wait to see you try, cowboy."

She slides out of the truck before I can respond, but not before I see the challenge burning bright in her eyes. As I watch her walk up to the porch, hips swaying with each step, I know I'm in trouble.

Big trouble.

But for the first time in years, it's the kind of trouble I'm looking forward to.

ELEVEN
AUBREE

I'M DRAGGIN' ass after we went to the bar last night, but it was much needed. To feel like myself again, to not be hiding from everyone and everything because of what my ex-boyfriend did to me. Last night I was more like the Aubree who left here, and less like the Aubree who tucked her tail between her legs and came back.

There are dark circles under my eyes and a tiredness lining my face, but both of them are good. I'm working hard and having fun.

Putting on my boots and grabbing a flannel to ward off the chilly morning air, I stomp down the stairs.

"Who's going to go today?" I can hear Truett and Jesse talking in not exactly hushed tones. "Everyone is working. We desperately need to hire some more hands."

"To do that, we need more money," Jesse argues quietly. "To get more money—"

"I know," Truett cuts him off.

The nosy part of me desperately wants to know what they're talking about, and why it's in riddles instead of plain English. I clear my throat as I walk over the threshold from the hallway into the kitchen. "Morning, y'all."

Both of them shut their mouths and glance at me. "Morning, Aubree." Truett strolls over to the coffeepot on the counter and pours me a cup.

My eyes travel over to where Jesse is standing. He's leaning against the butcher block countertop, long legs crossed in front of him, arms over his chest. Our gazes meet, and he gives me a slow smile. Heat creeps up my neck before I clear my throat and look over at Truett. "I couldn't help but hear that y'all might need someone to go and get something done today?"

"Yeah." Truett hands me my coffee mug. "There's a feed order that needs to get picked up, but everybody's busy. We can't put it off for much longer because we're almost out of feed."

"I can do it," I offer without thought. "It's been a long time, but I remember how to drive a truck."

The two of them share a glance, and it's as if they're weighing between each other if I'm capable of this. Eventually, Truett answers. "All right, I'll let them know you're on the way after we have breakfast."

The look that passes between them doesn't escape my notice. There's something they're not telling me, some weight they're carrying that goes beyond simple ranch business. I file it away for later, along with all the other little inconsistencies I've noticed since coming home.

Breakfast is simple: eggs, bacon, and toast that Cookie has

left warming in the oven. The three of us eat in relative silence, though I catch Jesse watching me more than once. Every time our eyes meet, I feel that same electric jolt from last night, the memory of his lips on mine making my skin flush with heat.

"You sure you're okay to handle the truck?" Truett asks as we finish up. "It's been a while since you've driven anything that size."

"I'll be fine," I assure him, though privately I'm a little nervous. It has been years since I've driven anything bigger than the sedan I had when I still lived at home. "How hard can it be?"

Jesse snorts, earning him a glare from me. "What's so funny?"

"Nothing," he says, but his green eyes are dancing with amusement. "Just remembering the time you tried to back Dad's truck up to the barn and took out half the fence."

"I was sixteen!" I protest, heat flooding my cheeks. "And that fence was in a stupid spot anyway."

"Uh-huh." He pushes back from the table, standing to his full height. Those long legs of his seem to go on forever, and I have to force myself to look away. "Just be careful, all right? Call if you need anything."

There's something in his tone. Concern? Protectiveness? It makes my heart skip. "I will."

An hour later, I'm behind the wheel of Truett's pickup, trying to remember everything I learned about driving a stick shift all those years ago. The truck lurches and jumps as I navigate out of the ranch, but eventually I get the hang of it.

The drive into town gives me time to think, to process everything that's happened since I came home. Jesse's kiss last night, the way it felt to be in his arms again, the promise in his voice when he said he'd steal my heart. Part of me wants to let him try, to give in to this pull between us that's always existed.

But the other part, the part that's still healing from Daniel's betrayal, warns me to be careful. I can't afford to get my heart broken again, especially not by Jesse. He has the power to destroy me completely, and I'm not sure I'm strong enough to survive that kind of devastation twice.

Grabbing my phone, I scroll through until I find Nora's name and quickly make the call, putting her on speaker.

"Well, well," her voice fills the cab. "Look who's calling to check up on me."

"Just making sure you got home okay last night," I lie, though we both know that's not the only reason I'm calling.

"Uh-huh. And this has nothing to do with wanting to know what happened between me and Truett when he drove me home?"

I can't help but smile. Nora knows me too well. "Maybe a little. So? Anything to report?"

There's a pause, and I can practically hear her grinning. "He kissed me."

My heart does a little skip of excitement for my friend. "And?"

"And what? That's it. Nothing else to report. He walked me to the door, kissed me good night like a perfect gentleman, and left."

"How was it?" I press, needing details.

"Amazing," she admits, and I can hear the smile in her voice. "God, Aubree, it's been so long since I felt anything like that. I'd forgotten what it was like to want someone."

I know exactly what she means. Last night with Jesse awakened something in me that I'd thought Daniel had killed. The desire, the need, the flutter of possibility—it's all rushing back with a vengeance.

"So what happens now?" I ask.

"I don't know," she sighs. "We'll see, I guess. What about you and Jesse? Don't think I didn't notice you two practically devouring each other with your eyes on the dance floor."

Heat floods my cheeks even though she can't see me. "It's complicated."

"It always is with you two. But Aubree? Don't let fear keep you from something that could be amazing. You've been hiding long enough."

Her words hit closer to home than I'd like to admit. I have been hiding—from Daniel, from the past, from the possibility of getting hurt again. But maybe it's time to stop running.

"I should go," I tell her as I see the sign for Grizzly River Feed and Seed ahead. "I'm about to pick up some feed for the ranch."

"Okay, but think about what I said. Love you, girl."

"Love you too."

I end the call and pull into the parking lot of the feed store. The place looks exactly the same as it did when I was a kid, with weathered wood siding, a tin roof, and a hand-painted sign that's seen better days. Some things never change in small towns.

The bell above the door chimes as I enter, and the smell hits me immediately: grain, hay, and leather mixed with something else I can't quite place. Behind the counter, an older man I don't recognize looks up with a friendly smile.

"You must be here for the Weber order," he says before I can speak.

"That's right. I'm Aubree."

"Figured as much. You look just like your mama did at your age." He comes around the counter, wiping his hands on his apron. "I'll get the boys to load you up. Shouldn't take but a few minutes."

While I wait, I wander around the store, looking at the various supplies and equipment. It's like stepping back in time, everything from bridles and saddles to chicken feed and garden tools. This place serves every need a rancher or farmer could have.

"Aubree Weber? Well, I'll be damned."

I turn to find a tall man in a sheriff's deputy uniform approaching me, and it takes me a moment to place him. When I do, I smile. "Noah Sanchez? Oh my god, hi!"

He grins and pulls me into a friendly hug. "It's Deputy Sanchez now, but yeah. How long has it been?"

"Too long," I say, meaning it. Noah and I went to high school together, though we ran in different circles. He was the quiet, studious type, while I was more interested in causing trouble with Jesse and his brothers. "I heard you joined the sheriff's department."

"Five years ago," he confirms, his dark eyes warm. "What about you? Last I heard, you were conquering the big city."

The question hits a sore spot, but I manage to keep my smile in place. "Living back here for a while. Helping out at the ranch."

Something flickers in his expression. Concern? Suspicion?

Before I can analyze it, one of the store employees calls out that my order is ready.

"Guess that's my cue," I say, starting toward the door.

"Aubree, wait." Noah catches my arm gently, his expression serious now. "Be careful, okay? There are rumblings about what's happening out at Grizzly River Ranch, and you don't want to be caught in the middle of it."

My blood chills. "What kind of rumblings?"

For a moment, I think he might actually tell me. Then he shakes his head, his jaw tightening. "I can't get into specifics. Just...be careful who you trust."

Before I can press him for more information, he reaches out and caresses my cheek, his touch gentle but his eyes intense. "I'd hate to see you get hurt, Aubree. You've always been too good for this place."

The gesture is intimate, unexpected, and I take a step back. "Noah, I..."

"Just think about what I said, okay?" He drops his hand and steps back, becoming the professional deputy again. "Take care of yourself."

He walks away before I can respond, leaving me standing there with more questions than answers. What did he mean about rumblings? What's happening at the ranch that I don't know about?

As I drive home, my mind races with possibilities. The cryptic conversation between Jesse and Truett this morning, their worry about money, Noah's warning...it all adds up to something bigger than I understood. Something potentially dangerous.

The question is: What am I walking into? And more importantly, how deep are Jesse, Truett, and our families involved in whatever it is?

By the time I pull back onto the main road and head toward the ranch, dark clouds are building on the horizon, and I have a sinking feeling that the storm approaching isn't just about the weather.

TWELVE
JESSE

"IT'S GETTIN' late. She should've been back by now," I mumble as Denver and I sit at the barn, waiting for Aubree to show up. We're here to unload the feed for her, but we've been waiting for over an hour. "Think something happened to her?"

Denver shakes his head. "Don't think so. Check out those clouds." He points to the west. "I think she's probably run into rain, and it's headed this way. Possibly a storm."

Why I didn't see it before, I'll never know, but he's right. There are black clouds building on the horizon. "Think we should give her a call and see what's happening?"

"That's up to you." Denver's tone is amused. "But I've never known you to be worried about a damn thing before."

I just don't let him see it. I worry about every fucking thing and have since we lost our parents. That's a trauma you never get over. Becoming responsible for your entire family within a few hours as a teenager. Stepping further into the barn so that I can have some privacy, I place a call to her cell. Hopefully, she hasn't changed the number in all these years.

When she answers, I can hear the pounding of the rain against the truck.

"Jesse?"

"Yeah, you okay? Shoulda been here an hour ago." I do my best not to let my tone be as gruff as I'd like for it to be.

"Ran into a storm, and the road is flooding. Should be home in the next thirty minutes or so. Won't be able to get this unloaded, though. They put a tarp over it before I left."

Nodding, I take off my gloves and put them in my back pocket. "All right, just head to the barn when ya get here. I'll be waiting, and we can ride out the storm."

"See you soon."

Denver looks over, his eyebrows raised. "What's the plan?"

"Head home," I instruct him. "Rain is coming, and if it's anything like it sounded hitting that truck, we ain't going out tonight anyway. Too easy to be caught with tire tracks and footprints. I'll help her when she gets here. Y'all head on out. Cookie's not making dinner tonight."

"You sure you don't need help?" he confirms before grabbing the keys to the truck.

"Positive. Go get your brothers and head to the house."

He salutes me before jogging to his truck and getting in. Once he takes off, all I do is sit and watch the drive for the headlights I know will be Aubree.

The first drops of rain start falling just as I see headlights cutting through the growing darkness. Right on time, as always. Even after all these years, Aubree's timing is impeccable.

I jog out to meet her as she parks near the barn, and by the time she's stepping out of the truck, the sky has opened up completely. Fat raindrops turn into a torrential downpour in seconds.

"Shit!" she yells over the sound of rain hammering the metal roof of the truck. "This came out of nowhere when I was on my way home."

"Come on!" I grab her hand, and we run for the barn, both of us soaked through before we make it five steps.

The barn doors are heavy, but I manage to get them open far enough for us to slip inside. The sound of rain on the tin roof is deafening, drowning out everything else.

We stand there for a moment, dripping and breathing hard. Aubree's honey-blonde hair is plastered to her head, and her flannel shirt clings to every curve of her body. She looks like a drowned rat, and she's still the most beautiful thing I've ever seen.

"Jesus." She laughs, pushing wet hair out of her face. "I haven't been caught in rain like that since I was a kid."

"You're soaked through," I observe, trying not to focus on how the wet fabric of her shirt has become nearly transparent. "And you're shivering."

She wraps her arms around herself, and I can see goose bumps rising on her skin. "A little. It's colder than I expected."

Without thinking, I step closer and start rubbing my hands up and down her arms, trying to generate some warmth through friction. The movement brings us close together, close enough that I can see the water droplets clinging to her eyelashes.

"Better?" I ask, my voice rougher than it should be.

She nods, but I can feel her trembling under my touch. "Still pretty cold though."

"We need to get out of these wet clothes," I say, then immediately realize how that sounds. "I mean, you'll catch pneumonia if you stay in wet clothes."

A smile tugs at the corner of her mouth. "Worried about me, Jesse Nelson?"

"Maybe." I don't see any point in lying about it. "Come here."

I lead her deeper into the barn, where we keep some old blankets for the horses. The space is warmer here, sheltered from the wind that's driving the rain against the walls.

"Your shirt," I say, gesturing to her flannel. "It's soaked through. You need to get it off."

For a moment, she just looks at me, something unreadable in her dark eyes. Then she reaches for the buttons, her fingers fumbling with the wet fabric.

"Here, let me." I step closer, my hands replacing hers on the buttons. My knuckles brush against her skin as I work each one free, and I feel her sharp intake of breath.

The flannel falls open, revealing a white tank top underneath that's just as wet and twice as revealing. I can see the outline of her bra, the soft curves of her breasts, and that heart-shaped birthmark I remember from our one night together all those years ago.

"Jesse," she whispers, and there's something in her voice that makes me look up at her face.

Her lips are slightly parted, her breathing shallow. The air between us feels charged, like the electricity from the storm outside has found its way into this barn.

"You're still cold," I murmur, though we both know that's not what this is about anymore.

"So are you." Her hands come up to rest on my chest, and I realize she's right. My shirt is just as soaked as hers was.

Before I can overthink it, I grab the hem and pull it over my head, tossing it aside. Her eyes widen slightly as she takes in the tattoos that cover my chest and arms, ink I've gotten since she's been gone, stories written on my skin that she doesn't know.

"You're different," she says, her fingertips tracing the outline of a tattoo on my collarbone.

"So are you." My hands find her waist, thumbs brushing just under the hem of her tank top. "But some things are exactly the same."

"Like what?"

"Like the way you make me feel like I'm losing my damn mind." The confession slips out before I can stop it, raw and honest in a way that leaves me feeling exposed.

Her breath catches. "Jesse..."

"I know we shouldn't," I say, pulling her closer until there's barely an inch of space between us. "I know it's complicated and messy and probably gonna end badly. But Christ, Bree, I can't stop thinking about last night. About dancing with you, kissing you..."

"Then don't stop," she whispers, and that's all the permission I need.

My mouth crashes down on hers, desperate and hungry. She responds immediately, her arms winding around my neck, her body pressing against mine. She tastes like rain and coffee and something uniquely her that I've never been able to forget.

I walk her backward until her back hits the wooden wall of the barn, my hands roaming over every inch of exposed skin I can find. She gasps when I kiss my way down her throat, her head falling back to give me better access.

"God, I've missed this," I murmur against her skin. "Missed you."

Her hands are everywhere, tangling in my hair, scraping down my back, tracing the lines of my tattoos. Every touch sets me on fire, makes me want to forget about everything else except the feel of her in my arms.

I'm reaching for the hem of her tank top when she suddenly goes rigid against me.

"Wait," she pants, her hands pressing against my chest. "Stop."

I freeze immediately, stepping back to give her space. "What's wrong? Did I hurt you?"

"No." She shakes her head, but I can see the confusion in her eyes. "No, you didn't hurt me. It's just..." She takes a shaky breath. "What did Noah mean?"

"What?" The question catches me off guard.

"At the feed store today. Noah Sanchez—he's a deputy now. He told me to be careful, that there were rumblings about what's happening at the ranch." Her eyes search mine, looking for answers I can't give her. "What did he mean, Jesse?"

Fuck. I knew this would happen eventually, but I was hoping for more time. Time to figure out how to explain things, time to prepare her for the truth.

"I don't know what you're talking about," I lie, but we both know it's bullshit.

"Don't." Her voice is sharp now, all the heat from moments ago replaced by suspicion. "Don't lie to me. I heard you and Truett this morning, talking about needing money and not being able to hire more hands. And now Noah is warning me about rumblings? What the hell is going on?"

I run a hand through my wet hair, trying to buy time to think. How do I explain that we're running cattle that don't belong to us? That we're stealing from other ranches to keep ours afloat? That everything we've built could come crashing down at any moment?

"There are things you can't know about," I finally say. "Things that are better left alone."

"Better for who?" she demands.

"For you. For your safety." I step closer again, my voice urgent. "Bree, please. Don't ask questions whose answers might get you hurt. Trust me on this."

She stares at me for a long moment, and I can see the war playing out in her expression. Part of her wants to trust me, to let this go. But the other part, the part that's always been too curious for her own good, won't let it drop.

"I can't do this," she says finally, pushing past me toward where she dropped her flannel shirt. "I can't get involved with someone who won't be honest with me. Not again."

"Aubree, wait..."

"No, Jesse." She pulls on the wet shirt with sharp, angry movements. "I came back here broken because a man lied to me, and I won't let that happen again. Whatever you're mixed up in, I can't be part of it."

She heads for the barn door, but I catch her arm. "The storm—"

"I'd rather get struck by lightning than stay here with someone who thinks I'm too weak to handle the truth."

The words hit me like a physical blow. "It's not about weakness. It's about keeping you safe."

"That's not your choice to make." She jerks free of my grip. "Thanks for the ride home last night. And for the dance. But this, whatever this is between us, it's over before it started."

She pushes through the barn doors and disappears into the storm, leaving me standing there half-naked and completely gutted. Through the rain, I hear the truck door slam, then the engine turning over.

I watch her taillights disappear into the darkness, and for the first time since my parents died, I wonder if trying to protect the people I love is actually destroying them instead.

THIRTEEN
AUBREE

I BURST through the front door of the big house, welcomed by the roar of a fire in the fireplace. At some point, Cookie's been here. Even though he's not making dinner for everyone, he took time out of his day to make sure I'd be warm when I get home.

I'm the only one who loves the fireplace.

It was the gathering spot for our family, and after my parents died, it hurt Truett to even look at it. I'm the one who wanted it blazing at any given chance. I'm the one who would sit in front of it and read books. It's the one thing I missed desperately while I was gone, and believe it or not, one of the main reasons I came home.

I needed familiarity and comfort, which is exactly what this fireplace represents.

The house is quiet. Has been since our parents died, and while this fireplace is my comfort, I hate the rest of the house. In every nook and corner, there are memories of what life was like before we lost them, what I wish we could still have. If only that drunk driver hadn't crossed the yellow line.

"Truett," I yell. "Are you here?"

I'm not surprised when he doesn't answer. If there's one thing I've learned since I moved back in, he's hardly ever here. Not wanting to be by myself, I pick up my phone and cross my fingers that I have service. When I see that it's connected, I place a FaceTime request to Nora.

She answers almost immediately. Her face is almost as familiar as my own.

"Hey, what's going on?"

I sigh and sit back against the couch. "Can you talk?"

"I'm in between patients. What's going on?"

I stare at the flames dancing in the fireplace, trying to figure out how to even begin this conversation. The warmth feels good against my skin, but there's a chill inside me that has nothing to do with the weather outside.

"Something weird happened today at the feed store," I finally say, tucking my legs underneath me. "Noah stopped me on my way out."

Nora's eyebrows raise. She knows Noah from high school, just like I do. "Deputy Sanchez? What did he want?"

"That's just it. He was acting all official and serious, not like the Noah we grew up with." I run my fingers through my honey-blonde hair, still damp from the rain. "He warned me about Truett and Jesse. Said they're into something dangerous and I should be careful."

The concern that flashes across Nora's face makes my stomach drop. She adjusts her position, and I can see she's in her office at the clinic, still wearing her scrubs.

"What exactly did he say?"

"He told me to watch myself around them. That they're not the same people they used to be." I pause, remembering the intensity in Noah's eyes. "Nora, he looked scared. Actually scared. And you know, Noah. Nothing rattles him. He used to stare down that o-line without fear."

"Aubree..." She hesitates, glancing around her office like someone might be listening. "I don't know anything for certain, but there's been talk around town."

My heart starts racing. "What kind of talk?"

"People have noticed things. Cattle going missing from ranches in surrounding counties. Always small numbers, nothing that would trigger a major investigation, but enough that folks are starting to connect dots." She lowers her voice. "And your brother and Jesse, they've been spotted in areas where it's happened."

I feel like someone just punched me in the gut. "Are you saying they're stealing cattle?"

"I'm saying you need to be careful. I know you love Truett, and I know there's history with Jesse, but if they're involved in something illegal..." She trails off, but I can see the worry etched on her face.

I think about all the times Truett has been gone lately, all the hushed conversations that stop when I walk into a room. The way Jesse looked at me tonight in the barn, not just with desire, but with something darker. Something desperate. Even going back to after our parents died. How did we make it?

"They wouldn't," I whisper, but even as I say it, doubt creeps in. "They're good men, Nora. They wouldn't resort to stealing."

"Good men do bad things when they're desperate," she says

softly. "And from what I hear, both ranches have been struggling since your parents died."

The fire crackles loudly, and I jump. Everything feels different now, like the walls of this house are closing in on me. The comfort I found here suddenly feels false, built on lies I didn't know existed.

"How bad is the talk?" I ask.

"Bad enough that people are starting to watch them. Bad enough that Noah felt he needed to warn you." She pauses. "Aubree, if they are involved in rustling, this isn't just about a few stolen cows. This is federal-crime territory. Prison time."

My hands shake as I process her words. Prison. The thought of losing Truett to something like this makes me sick. And Jesse... God, Jesse. After everything we've been through, everything we lost, how could they risk throwing their lives away?

"What am I supposed to do? Confront them? They'll just lie to me anyway."

"You could leave again," Nora suggests gently. "Come stay with me in town until this blows over."

"No." The word comes out stronger than I feel. "I just got home. I'm not running again."

"Then be smart. Keep your eyes open, don't ask too many questions, and whatever you do, don't get involved. If they are doing what people think they're doing, the last thing you need is to become an accessory."

The word accessory hits me like a slap. The idea that I could somehow be implicated in whatever they're doing makes my chest tight.

"There's something else," I admit, my voice barely above a

whisper. "Tonight in the barn, Jesse was...different. Intense. Like he was barely holding himself together."

"Different how?"

I think about the way his green eyes burned when he looked at me, the desperation in his touch when he pulled me against him. "Like a man with nothing left to lose."

Nora is quiet for a long moment. "Those are the most dangerous kind, Aubree. Men with nothing left to lose will do anything to protect what little they have left."

"He kissed me," I blurt out.

"What?"

"Jesse kissed me. And God help me, I kissed him back." I cover my face with my hands. "It was like all these years just disappeared, and I was eighteen again."

"Oh, honey."

"I know it's stupid. I know I should stay away from him, especially if what you're saying is true. But Nora, when he touched me, it felt like coming home."

"Listen to me very carefully," she says, her voice taking on that no-nonsense tone she uses when she's being serious. "Whatever you're feeling for Jesse, whatever history you two have, you cannot let that cloud your judgment. If he's involved in criminal activity, getting close to him will only drag you down with him."

I know she's right, but knowing and feeling are two different things. The memory of Jesse's hands on me, his mouth claiming mine, sends heat through my body even as fear chills my blood.

"I should have stayed in Chicago," I whisper.

"Maybe. But you're here now, and you have to deal with the reality of the situation." Her voice softens. "I love you, and I want you to be safe. That means keeping your distance from whatever Truett and Jesse are involved in."

A sound outside makes me freeze. Car doors slamming. Voices.

"Someone's here," I whisper.

"Who?"

I creep to the window and peek through the curtains. Truett's truck is in the driveway, but there's another vehicle too. Through the rain, I can make out two figures walking toward the house.

"It's Truett and Jesse."

"Aubree, listen to me. Act normal. Don't let them know you suspect anything. And for God's sake, don't be alone with Jesse."

"I have to go."

"Call me tomorrow. Promise me."

"I promise."

I end the call just as the front door opens. Truett walks in first, shaking rain from his jacket. Jesse follows, his dark hair wet, his green eyes immediately finding mine across the room.

"Hey, sis," Truett says, hanging his hat on the hook by the door. "Didn't expect you to be up."

"Couldn't sleep," I lie, my heart pounding. "The storm's pretty bad out there."

"Yeah, it is." He glances at me, his eyes closed off. A look I've seen before but never understood until now. "I was just checking on some fencing that might've come down." He's lying, and I know it.

The lie rolls off his tongue so easily, it makes me sick. How many other lies has he told me since I've been back?

"Everything okay?" he asks, his voice rough.

"Fine," I say quickly. Too quickly. "Just tired."

Truett takes a step closer, his gaze intense. "You sure? You look pale."

"I'm fine, Truett." I stand up, needing distance between us. "I'm going to bed."

As I walk past him toward the stairs, he reaches out. "Aubree."

I look up at him, and for a moment, I see my brother, the one who saved me from all the bad stuff. My hero when our parents died. Before life got complicated, before we lost everything that mattered.

"Get some sleep," he says softly, releasing my arm. "Things will look better in the morning."

Only this time, I don't believe him.

FOURTEEN
JESSE

I WATCH Aubree run away from me. Everything in my body is screaming to stop her, but I can't. There are things I have to do tonight to get prepared for our next job. Looking back at the feed sitting there, I sigh. It'll still be there tomorrow.

Truett comes into the barn, water dripping from the brim of his hat. "Are you ready? You got rid of Aubree?"

"Yeah, she's back up at the house. Pissed her off, so she's not coming to look for either of us for a while."

He laughs because he probably thinks I did it to keep her from being interested in where we're going tonight. He doesn't think about us actually having an issue with each other. Clapping me on the shoulder, he gives me a grin. "Good job. Now we don't have to lie. Well, at least until I get back to the house tonight."

Lying. It's what we've done since our parents died. It's what we've had to do. Those first few months and years were lean. No one knew how bad it was, though, because we didn't let on. I'll never forget how fucked we realized we were when we took a look at the financials for both of our ranches. Our parents were living on credit, and they owed everyone, which means we did too.

Needless to say, two young kids, trying to keep their families together, made decisions, and for better or worse, they're what have kept us going.

"Can you drive?" Truett asks. "Your dad's old truck still runs, and the last thing we need is for someone to see us."

"Yeah, let's head on out."

My dad's old truck stays in the garage behind the barn, just in case we need it. We both grab jackets and head out into the storm that's still raging.

The rain hits us like a wall as we make our way across the yard. Lightning illuminates the landscape in brief, stark flashes, and thunder rolls across the valley like God's own fury. Weather like this is perfect for what we're doing. It keeps honest folks inside and provides cover for those of us who aren't so honest anymore.

The garage door groans as I pull it open. Dad's old Chevy sits there like a sleeping beast, covered in dust and regret. I run my hand along the hood, remembering when he taught me to drive in this thing. Back when I thought I'd follow in his footsteps, be the kind of man who built things instead of stealing them.

"You getting sentimental on me?" Truett asks as he climbs into the passenger seat.

"Just thinking."

"Don't. Thinking gets us in trouble."

The engine turns over on the third try, rumbling to life with a deep growl that reminds me of better times. I back out into the storm, headlights cutting through the darkness as we head toward the county road.

"Tell me about the Morrison place again," I say as we drive.

"Three hundred head of Black Angus, mostly heifers. They graze the north pasture closest to the road." Truett pulls out a crumpled piece of paper with notes scrawled across it. "Old man Morrison's been in the hospital for two weeks with a heart attack. His son Jimmy's trying to run things, but he's green as grass and dumber than a fence post."

"Security?"

"One ranch hand lives on the property, but his trailer's on the south end, at least two miles from where we'll be working. No cameras that I could see when I drove by yesterday."

We've been planning this job for three weeks. The Morrison ranch sits in Jefferson County, just far enough away that no one would immediately suspect us, but close enough that we can get cattle moved and sold before anyone notices they're gone. It's not the first time we've done this, and it won't be the last.

The guilt eats at me sometimes, especially when I see the fear in other ranchers' eyes at the feed store or the diner. These are good people, hardworking folks just trying to make an honest living. But then I think about the stack of overdue bills on my kitchen table, the bank notices, the threat of losing everything my family built, and the guilt gets pushed down deep where it can't touch me.

"How many you thinking?" I ask.

"Ten, maybe twelve. Enough to make it worth our while, but not so many they'll be missed right away."

The windshield wipers fight against the rain as we drive

deeper into the countryside. This part of South Dakota is all rolling hills and barbed wire, ranch land that stretches to the horizon under normal circumstances. Tonight, the world ends twenty feet in front of our headlights.

"You ever think about what our parents would say if they could see us now?" I ask.

Truett is quiet for a long moment. "Every damn day. But they're not here to see the bills pile up or watch us lose everything they worked for. They're not here to figure out how to keep food on the table or make payroll for the hands. Not to mention, they left us with a fucking mess. What were we supposed to do?"

"We could have found another way."

"What way? You tell me, Jesse, because I've been racking my brain for years trying to find an honest solution." His voice gets sharp, defensive. "You think I like this? You think I wanted to become a cattle thief?"

I know better than to push him when he gets like this. Truett carries the weight of responsibility heavily on his shoulders, always has. When his parents died, he became the man of the house overnight, had to take care of Aubree and keep the ranch running. Just like me, only I think I handled it better.

"She suspects something," I say instead.

"Who? Aubree?"

"Yeah. Tonight in the barn, she was asking questions. Wanted to know where you've been going, why you're never home."

Truett rubs his face with both hands. "Shit. What did you tell her?"

"Nothing specific. But she's not stupid, Truett. She's going to figure it out eventually."

"Then we need to be more careful. The last thing we need is for her to get involved in this mess."

The thought of Aubree finding out what we've become makes my chest tight. Bad enough that I've turned into someone my father would be ashamed of, but for her to see it? To know that the man she once loved has become a criminal?

We drive in silence for the next thirty minutes, both lost in our own thoughts. The Morrison place comes into view as a cluster of lights in the distance, barely visible through the storm. I pull off the main road onto a dirt track that runs along the property line.

"This is it," Truett says, pulling out a pair of binoculars. "Cut the lights."

I kill the headlights and engine, and we sit in the darkness listening to the rain pound on the roof. Through the passenger window, I can make out the fence line and beyond it, the dark shapes of cattle huddled together under a stand of cottonwood trees.

"There they are," Truett whispers, though there's no one around for miles to hear us.

I take the binoculars and peer through them. Even in the dim light, I can see the cattle clearly. Black Angus, just like Truett said, quality stock that'll bring good money at the sale barn in Rapid City.

"How do you want to do this?"

"We're already here. Let's get this done. Cut the fence, move the cattle through. We load them in the trailer and get the hell out of here."

It sounds simple when he says it like that, but cattle rustling is anything but simple. You have to know which animals to take, the ones that won't be missed immediately. You have to move fast but quietly, get them loaded and transported before anyone realizes they're gone. And you have to have buyers lined up who don't ask too many questions about where the cattle came from.

We've all gotten good at it over the years. Too good.

"Let's make sure we've got all our bases covered. That they don't have security we don't know about," I mutter, reaching into the back seat for our gear. We'll take off on foot to check.

The rain soaks through my jacket within seconds of stepping out of the truck. We work quickly and silently, muscle memory guiding us through the familiar routine. Wire cutters slice through the fence, creating an opening just wide enough for cattle to pass through. Truett moves among the herd with practiced ease, making sure there's nothing that will let anyone know that someone is here who shouldn't be.

When we're done, we trek back to the truck. My clothes are soaked through, my boots caked with mud, and every muscle in my body aches from the constant tension of discovery.

"That's good," Truett calls out over the storm. "Let's go."

In the distance, headlights cut through the darkness. My blood turns to ice.

"Shit," Truett hisses. "Someone's coming."

We both drop low, using the truck to shield us from the approaching vehicle. Through the rain, I can see it's a pickup truck moving slowly along the road, spotlight sweeping the fence line like whoever's driving is looking for something.

Or someone.

"You think Morrison's boy is out checking cattle in this weather?" I whisper.

"In this storm? Not unless he's stupider than I thought."

The truck stops directly across from where we're hidden. The spotlight beam swings back and forth, probing the darkness. My heart hammers against my ribs so hard I'm sure whoever's in that truck can hear it over the thunder.

After what feels like an eternity, the truck moves on, taillights disappearing into the storm.

"Close one," Truett breathes.

Too close. We're getting sloppy, taking too many risks. But we don't have a choice, not if we want to keep our ranches.

The drive back is tense. Every set of headlights in the distance makes us both jump. Every siren in the far distance makes our blood run cold. We take back roads and farm tracks, staying off the main highways where possible.

We're almost home when the red and blue lights appear in the rearview mirror.

"Fuck," I breathe, my hands tightening on the steering wheel.

"Stay calm," Truett says, but I can hear the panic in his voice. "We're just two ranchers heading home after checking our property in the storm."

The patrol car follows us for another mile before hitting the sirens. I pull over on a wide spot next to a pasture gate, my mind racing.

"The gun," Truett whispers urgently.

Shit. The .38 we keep for protection is tucked under my seat. Having it while committing a felony turns this from simple rustling into armed robbery.

I reach down and grab the weapon, looking around frantically for somewhere to hide it. Finally, I shove it deep into the space between the seat and the door, praying it won't fall out.

The officer approaches through the rain, flashlight beam dancing ahead of him. Even before he gets close enough for me to see his face, I know who it is. The way he walks, the set of his shoulders.

Noah Sanchez.

"Shit," Truett mutters under his breath. "It's Noah."

Deputy Sanchez taps on my window with his flashlight. I roll it down, trying to look casual despite the fact that my heart is trying to beat its way out of my chest.

"Evening, Jesse. Truett." Noah's voice is carefully neutral, professional. "You boys are out late in this weather."

"Hey, Noah," I manage. "Just heading home after checking on some cattle. This storm's got them spooked."

His flashlight beam sweeps the interior of the truck, taking in our mud-caked boots, our soaked jackets. "Checking cattle where?"

"Our north pasture," Truett lies smoothly. "Had some fence that needed repair after that wind earlier."

Noah nods, but his eyes are sharp, suspicious. He's known us both since we were kids, played football with us in high school, and dated some of the same girls. He knows when we're lying.

"Mind if I take a look at your trailer?"

My blood turns to ice. "What for?"

"Routine check. You know how it is."

He knows. Somehow, he knows what we've been up to. Maybe he's been watching us, maybe someone tipped him off, but the way he's looking at us tells me this isn't a random traffic stop.

"Sure thing," Truett says before I can object. "Nothing back there but some fence repair supplies."

Noah walks around to the back of the trailer, and I catch Truett's eye in the mirror. We both know we're fucked. There's evidence of what we've done back there if he looks hard enough.

But when Noah shines his light through the slats of the trailer, he stops. Frowns. Walks around to the other side.

He studies the trailer for another long moment, then walks back to my window. "Jesse, I've known you since we were kids. Your dad was a good man, and I know you've been struggling since he died."

I don't say anything. There's nothing to say.

"I also know that desperate men sometimes make bad choices." His voice drops lower, more personal. "Whatever you boys are mixed up in, it's not too late to get out."

"I don't know what you're talking about," Truett says.

Noah looks at him, then back at me. "There's been cattle going missing from ranches all over this part of the state. Someone who knows what they're doing, someone who understands ranching."

The rain drums on the roof of the truck, filling the silence.

"I'd hate to see either of you throw your lives away," Noah continues. "Your parents were good people. They wouldn't want this for you."

"Are we free to go?" I ask, my voice hoarse.

Noah studies my face for a long moment, then steps back from the truck. "Drive careful. This storm's not letting up anytime soon."

I roll up the window and put the truck in gear, my hands shaking. In the rearview mirror, I watch Noah walk back to his patrol car, but he doesn't follow us when we pull away.

"Jesus Christ," Truett breathes once we're out of sight. "I thought we were done for."

"We might still be. He knows, Truett. He fucking knows."

"But he let us go."

"This time. What about next time?"

We drive the rest of the way home in silence, both of us lost in our own thoughts. When we reach the ranch, we unload the cattle quickly, getting them into a holding pen where they'll stay until we can transport them to the sale barn tomorrow.

It's nearly three in the morning by the time we're finished. The storm is finally starting to let up, though rain still patters against the barn roof.

"We need to be more careful," I say as we put away our gear.

"Or we need to stop."

I look at him in surprise. "You want to quit?"

"I want a lot of things, Jesse. I want my parents back. I want to be able to pay my bills without stealing. I want my sister to be safe." He runs a hand through his wet hair. "But wanting something and getting it are two different things."

"If we stop now, we lose everything."

"If we don't stop, we might lose more than everything. We might lose our freedom. Our lives."

I think about Noah's warning, about the suspicion in his eyes. He gave us a pass tonight, but he won't do it again. Next time, we won't be so lucky.

"One more job," I say finally. "We do this Morrison job, and that's it. That'll give us enough to make it through the winter, and then we reassess."

Truett nods reluctantly. "One more job."

As we walk back toward the house, I catch a glimpse of

movement in an upstairs window. A curtain falling back into place, a shadow disappearing.

Aubree was watching. Waiting for us to come home.

I wonder how much she saw. How much she suspects.

And I wonder how much longer we can keep lying to the people we love.

FIFTEEN
AUBREE

THERE'S no reason that Jesse and Truett should be getting home this late in the middle of a storm. They were gone much longer than they should've been. If what Noah hinted at is true, then maybe they were scouting out their next location.

The front door shuts downstairs, and I hear Truett's loud footsteps trudging up the stairs. Looking back outside, I watch as Jesse backs out of the drive. From here, I can see his taillights until he turns onto the main road, headed toward his own ranch.

Pulling my thumbnail in between my teeth, I glance at the clock. It's after midnight, but I need answers. I need him to see me for who I am now, and not who I was back then.

The rain is still coming down hard as I go back and forth in my mind about what I should do. My stomach is in knots, but I know one thing about myself. I ran from here, then I ran from Chicago. At some point, I have to stop running. At some point, I have to be a goddamn adult and face the fact that these boys stepped up and were the men of their families when no one else was. It would be so easy to let Truett continue to take the burden of everything, but it's not fair.

And to know exactly what's been going on? I have to ask.

Truett won't tell me, but I know Jesse. If I push him hard enough, he'll tell me everything.

Mind made up, I get dressed, throw on a raincoat, and rush down the stairs. Before I can talk myself out of it, I'm outside, in Truett's truck, and heading toward Jesse's house.

"Aubree, you better hope you don't regret this," I tell myself as I slow down to pull onto the gravel road that leads to Dark Skies Ranch.

I haven't been here in years, and since it's so late at night, there's no way for me to see much. I'm not entirely worried about it right now, either. All I want to do is talk to Jesse. As soon as I park, I open the door and hop down. That's when I'm pressed against the driver's door.

My heart hammers against my ribs as Jesse's body cages me against the cold metal of the truck door. The rain pounds down on us, soaking through my coat within seconds, but all I can focus on is the heat radiating from his chest pressed against mine. His green eyes are wild in the darkness, reflecting the distant porch light like a predator caught in headlights.

"Jesse." My voice comes out breathier than I intended. "I need to talk to you."

"At midnight? In a goddamn thunderstorm?" His hands are braced on either side of my head, his face inches from mine. Water drips from his dark hair onto my cheek. "You're gonna catch pneumonia out here."

"I don't care." I push against his chest, but he doesn't budge. "I know you and Truett are hiding something from me. Noah said—"

"Noah doesn't know shit." The words come out sharp, dangerous. Jesse's jaw ticks under his beard. "Whatever he told you, forget it."

"So there is something to forget now?" I arch an eyebrow, trying to ignore the way his proximity makes my skin tingle. "Just tell me the truth, Jesse. I'm not a child anymore."

He laughs, but there's no humor in it. "No, you're not. But you're still naïve as hell if you think you can handle the truth."

Rain streams down my face, mixing with the tears of frustration I refuse to let fall. "Try me."

"Why?" He leans closer, his breath hot against my ear. "So you can run again? Like you did before?"

The accusation hits like a slap. "That's not fair."

"Isn't it?" His voice drops to a growl. "You disappeared for years, Bree. Fucking years without a word to me. And now you waltz back here expecting us to trust you with our business?"

"I was eighteen!" The words tear from my throat. "After I kissed you, I was scared. I didn't know what the hell was expected of me. It's not like any of you wanted to help me."

"And we would've helped you." His forehead drops to rest against mine. "We would've done anything for you. But you didn't give us the chance."

The pain in his voice breaks something inside me. "I'm here now."

"Are you? Or are you just biding your time until you find another reason to bolt?"

"Stop." I grip the front of his soaked T-shirt. "Stop making me the villain. I came back because this is my home. Because you and Truett are my family, whether you want to admit it or not."

Something shifts in his expression, the hardness cracking just enough to let vulnerability slip through. "Bree..."

"Just tell me what's going on. Please." I search his eyes. "I can't stand being lied to anymore. I've had enough lies to last a lifetime."

He's quiet for a long moment, the only sounds the rain pounding against the truck and the distant rumble of thunder. When he speaks, his voice is raw. "You want the truth? Fine. Truett and I have been rustling cattle."

The admission hits me like ice water. "What?"

"I'm not proud of it. Most of the time, it's not from innocent ranchers," he says quickly. "From the bastards who've been squeezing out the small operations. The ones who think they can buy up everything and push families off land that's been theirs for generations." He licks at the rain on his upper lip. "Or from the small operations that have men who like to lay hands on their wives. We teach a lesson."

My mind reels. "Jesse, that's..."

"Illegal? Yeah, I know." His laugh is bitter. "But it's the only way to keep your ranch afloat. The only way to make sure Truett doesn't lose everything your family built."

"There has to be another way."

"There isn't." His hands come up to frame my face. "We've tried everything legal, Bree. Banks won't lend, markets are shit, and the big operations are driving prices so low that honest ranchers can't compete. So we take from those who have too much and make sure the little guys survive."

"You could go to prison."

"Better than watching everything die." His thumb traces across my cheekbone. "But now you know why we can't have you involved. Why we need you to stay away."

"No." The word comes out fiercer than I intended. "I'm not running this time. I'm not letting you and Truett carry this alone."

"Goddammit, Bree..."

"I mean it." I grab his wrists, holding his hands against my face. "I won't be pushed away again. Not by you, not by anyone."

He stares at me for a long moment, something dark and hungry flickering in his eyes. "You're gonna be the death of me, woman."

Before I can respond, his mouth crashes against mine. The kiss is desperate, angry, full of years of frustration and longing. I melt into him, my hands fisting in his shirt as he devours me like a man starved. The rain continues to pour down on us, but I barely notice. All I can feel is Jesse, his heat, his strength, the way he kisses me like he's trying to brand me as his.

When we break apart, we're both breathing hard. His green eyes are black with desire.

"We need to get inside," he rasps. "Before you freeze to death."

I nod, not trusting my voice. He takes my hand and pulls me toward the house, both of us running through the rain. By the time we reach the porch, we're both soaked to the bone and shivering.

Jesse fumbles with the keys, his hands shaking, whether from cold or something else, I can't tell. The moment the door opens, he pulls me inside and slams it shut behind us. We stand there dripping in his entryway, staring at each other.

"Bree," he starts, but I silence him with another kiss.

This time, I'm the one in control. I push him back against the door, my tongue sliding against his as I pour seven years of want into the kiss. He groans low in his throat, his hands tangling in my wet hair.

"Upstairs," I whisper against his lips. "Now."

He doesn't need to be told twice. In one smooth motion, he sweeps me up into his arms, carrying me like I weigh nothing. I wrap my arms around his neck, pressing kisses to his throat as he takes the stairs two at a time.

His bedroom is dark except for the lightning flashing outside the windows. He sets me down gently, his hands immediately going to the zipper of my raincoat. I help him shrug it off, then reach for the hem of his wet T-shirt.

"Are you sure about this?" he asks as I pull the shirt over his head. My breath catches at the sight of him, all lean muscle and intricate tattoos that I want to trace with my tongue. "Because once we do this, there's no going back."

Instead of answering, I reach behind me and unzip my dress, letting it pool at my feet. His eyes go wide, taking in every curve of my body in the dim light.

"Jesus, Bree." His voice is reverent as his gaze settles on the heart-shaped birthmark on my breast. "You're even more beautiful than I remembered."

Heat floods through me at the look in his eyes. "Then stop talking and touch me."

He doesn't need any more encouragement. His hands are

everywhere, skimming over my skin, reacquainting himself with every dip and curve. When his mouth follows the path of his hands, I arch beneath him, my fingers threading through his dark hair.

"I've wanted this for so long," he murmurs against my throat. "Even when I tried to hate you for leaving, I still wanted you."

"I never stopped wanting you either," I confess, gasping as his teeth graze the sensitive spot where my neck meets my shoulder. "Not once. Not since I was a teenager."

He lifts his head to look at me, his green eyes intense. "Then why did you leave?"

The question hangs between us, heavy with years of hurt and misunderstanding. I reach up to cup his face, my thumb stroking across his cheekbone.

"Because I was scared," I admit. "Scared of what I felt for you. Scared of being trapped in a life I wasn't ready for. Scared of disappointing everyone."

"You could never disappoint me." He presses a soft kiss to my palm. "You came back. That's all that matters now."

"Jesse..." I pull his face down to mine, kissing him with everything I have. This time, it's not desperate or angry. It's tender, full of promise and forgiveness and hope for what we might build together.

When we finally break apart, the storm outside has begun to quiet, the thunder growing more distant. Jesse's forehead rests against mine, our breathing slowly returning to normal.

"Stay," he whispers. "Don't run from me again."

I look into his eyes, seeing the vulnerability he's trying to hide, the fear that I'll disappear like I did before. But I'm not that scared eighteen-year-old anymore. I'm a woman who knows what she wants, and what I want is this, him, us, whatever future we can build together.

"I'm not going anywhere," I promise, sealing the words with another kiss.

Outside, the rain continues to fall, but inside Jesse's arms, I've finally found my way home.

SIXTEEN
JESSE

I GROAN DEEPLY the next morning when I wake up and Aubree is still in my arms. She's got her ass pressed against my cock, and it's standing at attention. The palm of my hand grazes down her front, stopping at the peaked nipple.

She moans, pressing the engorged tip into my flesh. When she pops her ass back, grinding against my length, I latch onto her neck and use my free hand to grip her thigh.

"Jesse," she says breathlessly.

"Yeah, you're not getting out of this bed yet." I push the words out of my tight throat, use my hand to lift her thigh, and then slide my cock home.

"Fuck..." She tosses her head back against my shoulder.

I take her lips, tongues twisting as I press my cock into her pussy, still wet with my cum from last night. Her hands are tangled in the sheets, pulling them as she anchors herself to push herself harder onto my length.

"You're so fuckin' hot," I growl, letting go of her thigh and moving my hand between her thighs. With the tip of my finger, I worry her clit, strumming a rhythm meant to make her come again.

With her head tilted against my shoulder, I can see her mouth is open, hissing as I bottom out and hold still for a split second before I turn her underneath me, and then mount her. My forearms shake as I come up on my knees and thrust so hard I could rip holes in the sheets.

"Oh god, Jesse. Don't stop," she breathes, her nose flaring.

"Look at me," I instruct her. "Look at me when I spill into you. Look at me when you come on my cock."

Those eyes of hers open, the brown depths wet with some emotion I don't want to name just yet. But I need her. I need her to tell me that I'm the one making her fall apart this way. "Who's making you come? Whose cock is owning this pussy?"

"Yours," she whines, pulling her bottom lip between her teeth. "Yours."

And that's when she lets go, her body tightening on mine. I can't hold it anymore. I come, shooting deep inside her, hoping with everything I have she's not on birth control. That I can make her mine forever. But that's a different conversation for a different day.

In the aftermath, we're quiet, and I lazily drag my finger up and down her arm.

When we've lain there for longer than we should've, she turns over, looking at me. "What were you and Truett doing last night? You didn't bring anything home. Be honest with me. I can't help you—or trust you—unless you're honest."

"I don't want you involved in any of this," I tell her, my

stomach aching at the thought of her getting caught up in the aftermath.

"Then y'all should've thought about that before this even started. Why did it start?"

I stare at the ceiling for a long moment, feeling the weight of everything pressing down on my chest like a boulder. The morning light filtering through the curtains casts long shadows across the room, and I can hear the distant sound of the guys heading to their trucks. The engines turn over, and they leave to head toward Grizzly River. Normal sounds of a normal morning on what should be a normal ranch. But nothing about our lives has been normal for a long time now.

"You remember when our parents died?" I finally ask, my voice rough.

She nods against my shoulder, her breath warm on my skin. "Of course I remember."

"What you don't know is what we found out after the funerals. About the money." I take a deep breath, steeling myself for what I'm about to tell her. "There wasn't any."

She lifts her head, those dark eyes searching my face. "What do you mean?"

"I mean, we were broke, Aubree. All of us. Your daddy, my daddy, they'd been struggling for years. The ranches were mortgaged to the hilt, there was no life insurance worth a damn, and the bank was breathing down our necks from day one." The words taste bitter in my mouth. "You know how all the smaller ranches around here have been selling to those big corporations? There's a reason for that. There's no help coming from anywhere. We were on our own. Me and Truett against the fuckin' world."

She's quiet, processing this information, and I can see the wheels turning in her head. I keep tracing patterns on her arm, needing the contact to ground me.

"So what did you do?"

"At first? We tried to do everything legal. Truett and I, we worked our asses off trying to make the numbers work. We sold equipment and cut expenses everywhere we could. But it wasn't enough. We needed cattle to sell, needed them fast, or we were going to lose everything our families had built."

The memory of those early days still makes my jaw clench. The desperation, the fear of failing everyone who'd been left in our care. "We needed about twenty more head to make our payment to the bank. Just twenty cattle to buy us some time to figure out a real solution."

"Where did you get them?"

"That's when things got...complicated." I roll onto my side to face her properly, needing to see her reaction. "We found ten head that had wandered off from their herd, looked like they'd been missing for months. Thing is, when cattle wander like that, sometimes the brands get weathered, hard to read."

Understanding dawns in her eyes, but she doesn't say anything yet.

"It wasn't hard to change those brands. Make them look fresh again. Took them to market, sold them as our own." I pause, watching her face carefully. "Made enough money to keep the bank happy for another month."

"Jesse..."

"I know how it sounds. But it worked, Aubree. It actually worked. And when you're drowning, when you're watching everything your family built about to disappear, you'll grab onto any lifeline you can find."

She sits up, pulling the sheet around herself, and I immediately miss the warmth of her skin against mine. "So you kept doing it."

"We kept doing it." I sit up too, running my hands through my hair. "Started small, always from the big corporations that were buying up land left and right. Figured they wouldn't miss a few head here and there. And they didn't, not at first."

The guilt that's been eating at me for years rises in my throat. "We told ourselves we were just taking back what those companies had stolen from smaller ranchers. That we were evening the score somehow. But the truth is, we were desperate, and it was easy money."

"How long have you been doing this?"

"Started right after the accident." I lean back against the headboard, suddenly feeling exhausted. "We've been careful, never taking too many at once, never hitting the same place twice in a row. But those big organizations, they've gotten wise. They've moved their cattle further out, hired more security. It's not as easy as it used to be."

She's looking at me like she's seeing me for the first time, and I hate it. But I also know she deserves the whole truth.

"We've been saving every penny. We've each decided to sell off portions of our land, both ours and yours, the parts that aren't central to the ranch operations. But we need one more job to set us up for the rest of the year, give us enough cushion to make this land sale work without going under before we find buyers."

"And that's what you were doing last night at the Morrisons."

"That's what we were doing last night at the Morrisons," I confirm. "Scouting. The Morrison Corporation bought out the old Fletcher place about six months ago, moved a decent-sized herd in there. We were seeing how many they had, what their security looked like, planning our route."

She's quiet for a long time, her eyes focused somewhere beyond me. I can practically hear her thinking, weighing everything I've told her against whatever she thought she knew about me, about us.

"You don't have to do this," she finally says, her voice soft but firm. "There has to be another way."

Something hot and fierce rises in my chest at her words. Not anger, exactly, but something close to it. Something that's been building for months as I've watched everything slip through our fingers despite our best efforts.

Before she can react, I reach out and wrap my hand around her throat, not squeezing, not hurting, but firm enough to make my point clear. Her eyes widen, but she doesn't pull away.

"Listen to me," I say, my voice low and steady. "Either we do this job, or we'll never be able to break away from this life. We'll be stuck in this cycle forever, always one step away from losing everything. I'm asking for you to understand, but I'm damn sure not asking for your permission."

Her pulse is racing under my palm, but her gaze doesn't waver from mine. There's something in her eyes—fear, yes, but also something else. Something that looks almost like respect.

"This isn't just about money anymore, Aubree. This is about proving that we're not victims of circumstance. That we can take control of our own destinies instead of waiting for someone else to save us or destroy us." My thumb strokes along her jawline, gentle despite the firmness of my grip. "Your parents and mine, they played by all the rules. They did everything they were supposed to do, and it got them nothing but debt and early graves."

"Jesse..."

"I'm not asking you to like it. Hell, I don't like it. But I am asking you to trust that I know what needs to be done to secure our future. To secure your future."

The weight of responsibility sits heavily on my shoulders. Not just for my own land, my own legacy, but for hers too. She's tied to this life, whether she admits it or not. And if I fail, if we lose everything, she loses everything too.

"This one job, and we're out. We take our share, sell the land we need to sell, and we go legitimate. Build something real and lasting instead of just surviving day to day."

I can see the conflict in her expression, the war between what she thinks is right and what she knows is necessary. It's the same war I've been fighting with myself since all this started.

"What if you get caught?"

"We won't get caught." My voice carries more confidence than I feel, but she needs to hear it. "We've been doing this for years without so much as a close call. We know what we're doing."

I don't mention the situation with Noah last night. She doesn't need to know about that.

"And if something goes wrong anyway?"

I release her throat, letting my hand slide up to cup her face instead. "Then at least we went down fighting instead of just rolling over and accepting defeat."

She leans into my touch, closing her eyes briefly. When she

opens them again, there's a resolution there that wasn't there before.

"How much do you need? From this one job?"

"Enough to make our land sales work. Enough to pay off the immediate debts and give us breathing room to build something legitimate." I pause, studying her face. "Why?"

"Because if this is really the last time, if this really gets us out of this hole we're in, then I need to know what we're risking everything for. I need to know the exact number that stands between us and freedom."

The fact that she's asking, that she's thinking in terms of *us* and *we*, sends something warm through my chest. Despite everything I've just told her, despite the moral complexity of what we've been doing, she's still here. Still willing to stand with me.

"Thirty thousand. That's what we need to clear our debts and have enough left over to make the land sales work without going under in the meantime."

She nods slowly, like she's doing calculations in her head. "And you think you can get that from one job?"

"The Morrison herd is big enough. If we're selective, take only the best cattle, we can make thirty thousand easy. Maybe more."

"When?"

The simple question hangs between us, loaded with implication. She's not trying to talk me out of it anymore. She's asking when, which means she's accepting it. Maybe not liking it, but accepting it.

"Soon. Within the next couple of days. Tonight, if we can make it work. We need to move while the conditions are right, before they change their security protocols or move the herd again."

She's quiet again, and I can see her processing everything, weighing the risks against the potential rewards. It's the same calculation Truett and I have been making for months, but somehow having her go through it too makes it feel more real, more significant.

"I don't want to know the details," she finally says. "I don't want to know when exactly, or how, or any of it. But Jesse?" She looks directly into my eyes. "If this goes wrong, if something happens to you or Truett, I'll never forgive either of you for leaving me to pick up the pieces alone."

"Nothing's going to happen to us."

"You can't promise that."

She's right, and we both know it. But I can promise something else.

"I can promise that everything we're doing, every risk we're taking...it's all for this. For us. For the chance to build something together that nobody can take away from us."

She leans forward, pressing her forehead against mine. "Just promise me that after this job, that's it. No more. Whatever happens, we find another way."

"I promise."

And I mean it. This one job, and then we go clean. We sell the land, pay off the debts, and start over with whatever we have left. It might not be much, but it'll be honest, and it'll be ours.

She kisses me then, soft and sweet, and for a moment I can almost believe that everything is going to work out exactly the way we've planned. That in a few weeks we'll be free and clear, building a legitimate future together.

But as I pull her closer, as she melts against me in the morning light, I can't shake the feeling that we're balanced on a knife's edge. One wrong move, one piece of bad luck, and everything we're fighting for could disappear in an instant.

Still, as her hands slide up my chest and her lips find mine again, I know I'd make the same choice. Because sometimes the only way forward is through the darkness, and sometimes you have to be willing to risk everything to gain anything at all.

SEVENTEEN
AUBREE

TWO HOURS LATER, Jesse and I arrive at Grizzly River Ranch. Truett is sitting on the front porch, looking fit to be tied.

"Where the hell have you been?" he questions, his voice as angry as I've ever heard it.

"With Jesse," I answer. There's no shame in that statement, and I'm not expecting what happens next.

Truett gets up, strides across the gravel, and takes a good look at Jesse. He doesn't flinch as Truett looks him up and down. The glare is enough to frighten me, but Jesse doesn't back down. "My fuckin' sister? You could have anyone, and it had to be my fuckin' sister?"

Jesse shakes his head, his Adam's apple bobbing as he swallows roughly. "Yeah, it's always been your sister."

Before those words make it completely out from between his lips, Truett's fist meets his face.

"Truett!" I scream. "He's your best friend."

"And you're my sister. He knows you're off-limits."

Jesse doesn't fall, but he's knocked so that his back is resting against the pickup truck. It's holding him up as he struggles to get his bearings. "It was always her," Jesse says again, shaking his head. "You knew it, I knew it, and so did she."

Truett pulls back again, but I rush forward, grabbing hold of his forearm. "Please stop, please," I beg, my voice smaller than I mean for it to be. There are tears pooled in my eyes, and I'm trying desperately to hold on to them. I don't want Truett to see me as his little sister who can't handle the hard things. It's why he never told me about the trouble the ranches were in to begin with.

"He knows how I feel about you. He never should've looked twice at you, Aubree. Judging from the hickey on your neck and the fact you're still wearing the clothes you left here in last night, he's done much more than that."

I can't deny it. It'd be stupid to. "I'm also a grown-ass woman who knows what I want. You're not my dad, Truett. No matter the situation we were dealt."

"I've acted like it," he argues.

"And I've let you. That's my fault. I should've never let you take that much responsibility. You were a kid, just like me. Maybe over the age of eighteen, but you were still a kid. Both of you were." I lick my lips, my eyes going to Truett's. "And we've had so much loss in our lives, True. I always come back to Jesse. Regardless of whether you like it or know it, I always do. Let me have some joy and happiness."

"I know who he is," Truett says quietly. "He'll hurt you."

"Life has hurt me. He can't do anything that life hasn't already done, True. Let me have the joy before this life goes dark and there's no chance for any of us. Can you please do that?" I plead, breathless. "For me. Can you do that for me?"

"I'll do it for you." He pushes the words out between gritted teeth. "Not for him, but I'll do it for you."

Reaching up, I cup his cheek with the palm of my hand. "That's all I ask, True. If he hurts me, I'll let you handle it."

He turns to Jesse. "You know I'll fuckin' handle it and you. Watch yourself. Best friend or not, I will end you."

Jesse spits blood, wiping at his cheek. "I'd expect nothing less."

The three of us head inside, the tension thick enough to cut with a knife. Truett's jaw is still set in that hard line I know means trouble, while Jesse holds a bandana to his split lip. The silence stretches between us as we settle into the living room, Truett in Dad's old recliner, Jesse on the couch, and me perched on the edge of the coffee table between them like some kind of mediator. In the background, the fireplace, which has always brought me comfort, stands like a beacon in a storm.

"We need to talk," I say, breaking the quiet. "Jesse told me about the job you two are planning."

Truett's head snaps toward Jesse so fast I'm surprised he doesn't get whiplash. "You told her? What the fuck, man? The whole point was keeping her out of this."

"Don't blame him," I interrupt before Jesse can respond. "I asked him not to lie to me anymore. About anything. He was respecting that."

"Respecting that?" Truett's voice climbs an octave. "Aubree, this isn't some game. This is dangerous shit, and the less you know, the safer you are."

I stand up, crossing my arms. "I'm already in danger, Truett.

We all are. The ranch is failing, we owe money we don't have, and, apparently, there are people who want to hurt us. Keeping me in the dark doesn't make me safer. It makes me unprepared."

Jesse finally speaks up, his voice rough. "She's right, True. She deserves to know what's happening in her own life."

"This is exactly why I didn't want this to happen," Truett says, gesturing between Jesse and me. "Now you're taking her side over mine."

"There are no sides here," I say firmly. "We're family. All of us. And family doesn't lie to each other, no matter how good the intentions."

Truett runs both hands through his hair, a gesture so familiar it makes my chest ache. He's done that since he was little whenever he felt overwhelmed. "Fine. We're doing the Morrison job, and now you have no plausible deniability."

The words hit me like a physical blow. "I knew you were, but you know..."

"Dangerous as hell, I know," he continues. "Which is why I'm not putting you in any more danger than you already are. But I can make sure we let you know when we're safe."

My heart hammers against my ribs. "When are you doing this?"

Truett looks at Jesse, something passing between them in that silent communication they've perfected over years of friendship. "Tonight."

"Tonight?" The word comes out as barely a whisper.

"Which means we need you to do something normal," Truett continues. "Something that throws attention off of us. Be seen around town, establish an alibi."

I nod, my mind already racing. "I'll call Nora. Ask if she

wants to go shopping this afternoon, maybe have dinner together."

"Perfect," Jesse says, and when our eyes meet, there's something there—relief mixed with worry. "Just act normal. Don't do anything that might draw attention."

I pull out my phone and dial Nora's number, putting it on speaker so the guys can hear.

"Hey, girl!" Nora's cheerful voice fills the room. "What's up?"

"I was wondering if you wanted to go shopping this afternoon? Maybe grab dinner after? I'm going a little stir-crazy out here."

"Yes! This week has been crazy at the vet's office. Want to meet at Murphy's?"

Murphy's General Store is the only real shopping option in Grizzly River, unless you count the gas station's limited selection of toiletries and snacks. "Sounds perfect. What time?"

"How about two? We can browse around, maybe grab some of those cookies Mrs. Murphy makes, then head to the diner for an early dinner."

"Perfect. See you then."

After I hang up, Truett nods approvingly. "Good. That'll keep you visible and accounted for."

The next few hours crawl by. I try to act normal, but normal feels impossible when the two most important men in my life are about to risk everything on a plan that could get them arrested, or worse, killed. Jesse helps Truett with some repairs on the barn roof, and I busy myself with laundry and cleaning, anything to keep my hands occupied and my mind from spiraling.

At quarter to two, I change into clean jeans and a sweater, tie my hair back, and drive into town. Grizzly River looks the same as always, a main street lined with weathered storefronts, pickup trucks parked at angles, and the general sense that time moves a little slower here than everywhere else.

Nora is already waiting outside Murphy's when I pull up, her red hair caught up in a messy bun and a bright smile on her face. "There's my mysterious friend," she says as I approach. "You've been scarce lately."

"Just dealing with ranch stuff," I tell her, which isn't exactly a lie.

We spend the next hour wandering Murphy's aisles, picking through the limited selection of clothes, books, and household goods. Nora chatters about her job at the vet, her mother's latest attempts at matchmaking, and the gossip floating around town. I try to focus, to respond appropriately, but my mind keeps drifting to what Jesse and Truett might be doing right now.

"Oh, look who's here," Nora says, nudging me toward the small pharmacy section at the back of the store.

Behind the counter, counting pills into bottles with careful precision, is Atlee, Lennon's little sister. She's twenty-one now, with the same dark hair as her sister but a sharper jawline and a more serious expression.

"Hey, Atlee," I call out, and she looks up with a smile.

"Aubree! Nora! How are you two?"

"Good," I say, moving closer to the counter. "How do you like working here?"

"It's not bad. Keeps me busy, and it's good money. I'm trying to figure out if I want to go all in on pharmacy or not." She holds up a bottle of pills. "Right now, I'm mostly just doing inventory and basic stuff, but it's interesting."

"That's great," Nora says. "You always were good with details."

We chat for a few more minutes about her work, her brother's new job in Billings, and the general happenings around town. It's normal, mundane conversation, but I'm grateful for it. It makes me feel anchored to something real and stable.

My phone buzzes in my pocket, and I pull it out to find a text from Jesse.

> **J**
> Heading out now.

My blood turns to ice water in my veins. They're really doing this. Right now, while I'm standing here talking about pharmacy certifications and town gossip, Jesse and Truett are driving toward what could be the most dangerous night of their lives.

"You okay?" Nora asks, studying my face with concern. "You look like you've seen a ghost."

"Just tired," I manage to say, slipping my phone back into my pocket. "Maybe we should head to the diner?"

We say goodbye to Atlee and make our way back to the main street. As we're walking toward the diner, I catch sight of a familiar vehicle parked across the street—Noah's squad car. He's sitting behind the wheel, talking on his radio, and something about his posture makes my stomach clench with dread.

"Nora," I say, trying to keep my voice casual. "What do you think Noah's doing over there?"

She glances over and shrugs, looking at me as if I've lost my mind. "Probably just routine patrol stuff. You know how quiet it gets around here. He's probably bored out of his mind."

But I don't think it's routine. There's something alert about the way he's sitting, something focused about his attention that speaks of more than boredom. My phone feels heavy in my pocket, Jesse's message burning in my mind like a brand.

The bad feeling that's been lurking at the edges of my consciousness all day suddenly roars to life, settling in my chest like a living thing with claws and teeth. Something is wrong. Something is very, very wrong.

"Actually," I say, grabbing Nora's arm, "let's step it up. I'm starving."

I need to get us somewhere public, somewhere normal, somewhere with other people around. Because if my instincts are right, if Noah knows something, if this whole plan is about to go sideways, I need to be exactly where I'm supposed to be when it all falls apart.

As we walk into the diner, the little bell above the door chiming our arrival, I send up a silent prayer to whatever gods might be listening. *Keep them safe. Please just keep them safe.*

But the feeling in my gut tells me it might already be too late.

EIGHTEEN
JESSE

I'M nervous the entire day, especially when I watch Aubree leave. No job has ever meant so much as this one does. She knows what we're doing now, and the gravity of all of it is enough to send pain shooting through my sternum. Reaching up, I rub at the ache.

None of this feels good. Not that it ever does, but there's a definite finality hanging in the air.

Maybe it's because we've decided this will be the last hit, maybe it's because we're getting too damn old for all this. Either way, our luck is running out. We all have to know that.

"Are you okay?" Truett asks as we all meet in the barn.

All hands are on deck for this. Carson, Devlin, Denver, and Austin are all here, along with me and Truett. Everyone is cleaning their guns, and I notice that almost everyone has a knee that's bouncing up and down.

"Yeah, just ready to get this over with. It doesn't feel good," I whisper to him.

"I know. I'm trying to decide whether that's because Aubree knows now, or if we're just walking into what could be a trap." He rubs at his jaw. "Bottom line is we have to do it, though."

"Don't I know it."

We hold off until dusk settles along the horizon, and then we load up into three trucks with trailers. This is going to be our biggest take yet. Each truck and trailer will have two people with them. Truett and I, Devlin and Carson, and then Denver and Austin. These are my brothers. They are literally men I've walked into battle with. We've become almost as tight as a military unit over the years, and that will do nothing but help our cause tonight.

One last time, we each check our weapons, Truett confirms the plan, and we're off.

The Morrison place sits about forty miles southeast of the ranch, tucked into a valley that's perfect for what we need to do. Remote enough that screaming won't carry, but accessible enough that we can get our trailers in and out without getting stuck if we need to move quickly. It's different looking now than it was the other night when we came out for our reconnaissance mission. Quieter, more serious.

The drive is tense and almost silent. Truett's hands are steady on the wheel, but I can see the muscle in his jaw working overtime. Neither of us speaks much. There's not much left to say. We've gone over the plan a dozen times. Get in, get the cattle, get out. Simple in theory, complicated as hell in practice.

"Radio check," Truett's voice crackles through the comm system we've rigged between the trucks.

"Copy," comes Devlin's voice.

“Good here,” Denver responds.

We’re about five miles out when Truett kills the headlights. The other trucks follow suit. From here on out, it’s all about stealth and night vision. The moon is barely a sliver tonight, which works in our favor.

The Morrison property is spread out over several hundred acres, but we know exactly where the cattle are. Old man Morrison keeps his prize Angus in the north pasture, close enough to the house to keep an eye on them, but far enough away that we can work without being seen from the windows.

Truett parks our rig behind a stand of cottonwoods, and I can see the other trucks taking their positions. Everything is going according to plan so far.

“Remember,” Truett’s voice comes through the radio, barely above a whisper. “We’re looking for the thirty-three head in the north pasture. Nothing else. We get them loaded, and we get the hell out of here.”

“Copy that,” I respond, checking my rifle one more time. The weight of it feels heavier tonight, like it knows this is the last time I’ll be carrying it for this kind of work.

We move like shadows across the field, our boots making barely a sound on the frost-covered grass. Even in spring, we have to worry about cool temps. Years of doing this have taught us how to move without disturbing the world around us. Carson and Devlin head toward the fence line to start cutting through the wire, while Denver and Austin position themselves as lookouts.

The cattle are exactly where we expected them to be, clustered together in the center of the pasture, their warm breath creating little clouds in the cold night air. These are beautiful animals—prime beef stock worth a good amount of money per pound. It almost makes me feel guilty. Almost.

Truett and I approach the herd slowly, making soft clicking sounds with our tongues to get their attention without spooking them. Cattle are surprisingly intelligent animals, and if you know what you're doing, you can guide them almost anywhere.

"Easy, girl," I murmur to a particularly large cow who's eyeing me suspiciously. "We're just going to take a little walk."

The fence cutting goes smoothly, and within minutes, we have a clear path from the pasture to our trailers. Carson gives us the thumbs up, and we start the delicate process of moving the cattle.

This is where years of experience pay off. We've learned to work as a unit, each man knowing his role without needing to be told. Truett and I guide the lead animals toward the opening, while Carson and Devlin work the sides to keep any stragglers from wandering off. Denver and Austin have moved closer to the trailers, ready to help funnel the cattle up the ramps.

The first few animals are always the hardest. Cattle are creatures of habit, and they don't like being moved in the dark. But once you get a few of them moving in the right direction, the rest tend to follow.

"That's it," Truett whispers as the first cow steps through the cut fence. "Nice and easy."

One by one, the cattle file through the opening and toward our trailers. It's almost peaceful, in a way. Just the sound of hooves on grass and the occasional low moo from one of the animals.

We're about halfway through loading the final trailer when everything goes to hell.

The first shot comes out of nowhere, the muzzle flash lighting up the darkness like lightning. The bullet whizzes past my head close enough that I can feel the heat of it.

"Contact!" Truett shouts into his radio, diving behind the nearest trailer.

More shots follow, coming from multiple directions. Morrison must have figured out what we were up to, or maybe he just got lucky and couldn't sleep tonight. Either way, we're in deep shit.

The cattle scatter at the sound of gunfire, their earlier docility forgotten as panic takes over. Several of them bolt back toward the pasture, while others mill around in confusion between the trailers and the fence line.

"Return fire!" Truett orders, and suddenly the night explodes with the sound of gunshots.

I can see muzzle flashes from the direction of the house, and what looks like at least three different positions. Morrison didn't come alone. He brought backup.

I find cover behind the wheel of our truck and start laying down suppressing fire toward the house. The rifle kicks against my shoulder with each shot, and I can smell the acrid scent of gunpowder mixing with the cold night air.

"We need to move!" Carson's voice crackles through the radio. "They've got us pinned down!"

He's right. Our position is shit, caught out in the open with nowhere to go but back to the trucks. The cattle are scattered all over hell and creation, and we're taking fire from multiple directions.

"Get the animals that are already loaded and let's go!" Truett shouts.

But even as he says it, I know we're not going to make it out clean. There are too many of them, and they know this terrain better than we do.

I'm laying down covering fire when I hear Truett cry out. I spin around to see him stumbling backward, his left hand pressed against his right shoulder. Dark blood is seeping between his fingers.

"Truett!" I abandon my position and sprint toward him, keeping low to avoid the bullets that are still flying overhead.

He's gone pale, sweat beading on his forehead despite the cold. "I'm okay," he says through gritted teeth, but the amount of blood tells a different story.

"Like hell you are." I help him behind the cover of our truck and take a quick look at the wound. The bullet went through the meat of his shoulder, missing the bone but tearing up a lot of muscle and probably nicking an artery based on the amount of bleeding.

"We need to get out of here," he says, trying to push himself up.

"We need to get you to a doctor." I press my hand against the wound, trying to stem the bleeding. "Carson! We need to go... now!"

More gunfire erupts around us, and I can hear Denver shouting something about getting the trailers moving. The cattle that are loaded are bellowing and trying to break down the trailer walls, spooked by all the noise and chaos.

"Jesse, just leave me and get the cattle," Truett says, his voice getting weaker.

"Not happening." I key my radio with my free hand. "We're pulling out now."

"Negative," comes Devlin's voice. "We can still get the last of them loaded if we—"

"I said we're pulling out!" I cut him off. "That's an order!"

The next few minutes are a blur of gunfire, shouting, and controlled chaos. Carson and Denver manage to get their trailer loaded with about half the intended cattle, while Austin helps me get Truett into the passenger seat of our truck before he leaves in his own.

The bleeding isn't stopping, and Truett's getting weaker by the minute. I need to get him help, and I need to get it fast.

We peel out of there with bullets still flying, our trailers bouncing over the rough ground as we race back toward the main road. I can see headlights in my rearview mirror. Morrison and his boys are giving chase.

"How you doing, brother?" I ask Truett, who's slumped against the passenger door.

"Been better," he manages, but his voice is barely above a whisper now.

I push the truck harder, taking corners that I probably shouldn't at speeds that would make my insurance company weep. The trailer behind us fishtails on a particularly sharp turn, but somehow stays upright.

The chase doesn't last long. We lose them after about ten miles, but that doesn't make me feel any better about Truett's condition.

His breathing is getting shallow, and the makeshift bandage I've pressed against his shoulder is soaked through with blood. He needs real medical attention, and he needs it now.

I grab my phone with one hand, keeping the other on the wheel as we race through the darkness. I know I shouldn't be calling her—bringing Aubree further into this mess is the last thing I want to do—but she's the closest thing we have to medical help.

The phone rings once, twice, three times. Come on, Aubree, pick up.

"Jesse?" Her voice is slightly slurred, and I can hear music and laughter in the background. I recognize the noise. She's at the Rusty Spur, probably with the girls.

"Aubree, I need your help." I try to keep the panic out of my voice, but I'm not sure I succeed. "We need help, and we need it quick."

The background noise fades as she moves somewhere quieter. "What happened? Are you hurt?"

"It's Truett. He's been shot, and he's losing a lot of blood. We're heading back to the ranch now, but I don't know if I can get him to a hospital in time."

There's a pause, and I can almost hear her mind working. "How bad is it?"

I look over at Truett, whose eyes are closed and whose breathing is getting more labored. "Bad. Really bad."

"Okay, listen to me. I'm bringing Nora, and we'll meet you at the ranch. Do you have anything to stop the bleeding?"

"I've got pressure on it, but it's not enough."

"Keep the pressure on and try to keep him conscious if you can. We'll be there as soon as possible."

"Aubree—"

"Don't," she cuts me off. "Don't you dare apologize or try to explain right now. Just get him home alive, you hear me?"

The line goes dead, and I toss the phone aside. Ahead of me, I can see the lights of the other trucks. Carson's voice crackles through the radio.

"How's he doing?"

I look over at Truett again. His skin is gray, and there's blood on his lips now. That's not a good sign.

"Not good," I admit. "We need to get to the ranch fast."

"Copy that. We're right behind you."

I didn't even notice they've taken position to keep us safe on the road. The next twenty minutes are the longest of my life. Every time Truett's breathing gets more shallow, every time his head lolls forward, I'm sure I'm going to lose him. But somehow, he hangs on.

"Stay with me, brother," I keep saying. "Aubree's coming. She's going to fix you right up."

Truett's eyes flutter open at the mention of her name. "She shouldn't...be involved..." he whispers.

"Yeah, well, too late for that now."

The lights of Grizzly River Ranch finally come into view, and I've never been so happy to see home in my life. I can see headlights already in the driveway. Aubree and Nora beat us here.

I pull up right in front of the house, not caring about the gravel I send flying. Carson and the others are right behind me, their trailers still loaded with stolen cattle, but that's a problem for later.

Aubree comes running out of the house before I even have the truck in park. She's changed out of whatever she was wearing at the bar into jeans and a sweater, her honey-blonde hair pulled back in a ponytail. Behind her, I can see Nora carrying what looks like a medical bag.

"How is he?" Aubree asks as I jump out of the driver's side.

"Unconscious. Lost a lot of blood." I run around to the passenger side and carefully open the door. Truett's head is lolled back against the headrest, and for a terrifying moment, I think we're too late.

But then I see his chest rising and falling, shallow but steady.

"Help me get him inside," Aubree says, all business now. The woman who was probably laughing with her friends an hour ago is gone, replaced by someone who knows exactly what needs to be done.

Together, we manage to get Truett out of the truck and into the house. Nora has already cleared off the kitchen table and spread clean towels across it.

"Put him here," she directs, and we carefully lay Truett down on his back.

Nora immediately starts cutting away his shirt to get a better look at the wound. Her hands are steady and sure, and I'm reminded that although she's just a vet tech, we all have a lot of different experiences out here in these rural areas.

"The bullet went through," she says after a quick examination. "That's good. No need to dig it out. But it nicked something on the way through. He's lost a lot of blood."

"Is he going to be okay?" I ask, even though I'm not sure I want to hear the answer.

Nora looks up at me, her deep brown eyes serious but not panicked. "I don't know yet. But we're going to do everything we can."

As she and Aubree get to work, I step back and let them do

what they do best. Outside, I can hear Carson and the others unloading the cattle and trying to get them secured. The whole job was a disaster, but at least we got something for our trouble.

But looking down at Truett's pale face, I can't help but think that no amount of money is worth this. We should have quit while we were ahead.

The problem is, it might already be too late for regrets.

NINETEEN
AUBREE

MY HANDS ARE SHAKING as I help Nora work on my brother.

"We need medicine." She winces as she works to stitch up his wound. "If we don't get him some antibiotics and painkillers, he's going to be in a world of hurt."

"Where can we get it?" I question, going over every option we have at this time of night in a town as small as Grizzly River. It hits me like a Mack truck. "Atlee. She can get it for us."

Nora squints. "I don't want to get her in trouble, but she does owe me. It would be pretty easy for her to fudge records too, especially since she's been doing inventory. I know she went in late the other night to start on it when no one was there."

Grabbing my cell, I search through forgotten contacts until I get to Atlee. Pressing send on the call, I wait for the call to connect and then pick up.

"Aubree?" she questions. We left her back at the bar. She has no idea the shitstorm we're dealing with. "Where'd y'all go?"

"We have a problem," Nora says, her voice thick with authority. "We need painkillers and antibiotics. There's been an accident on the Grizzly River Ranch."

Atlee gasps. "Is everyone okay?"

Nora and I glance at each other. "They will be," I answer, my voice firm, no room for doubt.

"But we need that medicine tonight. If we send someone, can you help us get it?" Nora asks, reaching up with the back of her hand to wipe the sweat from her brow.

"Yeah, yeah," Atlee confirms. "I can get it."

"I'll go," Devlin says from where he's standing at the front door. I didn't even know he was here, but his large presence is comforting, knowing that Atlee will be in good hands.

Nora nods. "Devlin Nelson will meet you. Hurry."

Atlee's voice is breathless. "On it."

"Thank you," I tell her, hoping that she can hear the sincerity in my voice as I hang up the phone.

Then I turn and watch my best friend work on my brother, trying to keep him alive. Strong arms wrap around my neck and hold me close. Jesse fits his front to my back, widening his stance to keep me upright when I threaten to tip over.

The warmth of his body against mine is the only thing keeping me from completely falling apart. I can feel the tension in his muscles, the way his breathing has turned shallow and uneven. He's as terrified as I am, maybe more. Truett isn't just my brother. He's Jesse's best friend, his partner in every sense that matters on this ranch.

I close my eyes and lean back into Jesse's solid chest, letting his strength anchor me as memories flood back unbidden. I'm seventeen again, curled up in my bed, when Truett's heavy footsteps echo down the hallway at three in the morning. The way he knocked so softly on my door, like he was afraid to wake me, even though he needed to deliver the worst news of our lives.

"Aubree?" His voice had been broken, raw with grief I'd never heard from him before. "Aubree, I need you to wake up."

I remember how my heart had started racing before I even opened my eyes, some primal instinct telling me that whatever brought my big brother to my room in the dead of night wasn't good. When I sat up and saw his face in the dim light from the hallway, his eyes red-rimmed, his usually steady hands shaking, I knew our world had just changed forever.

"There's been an accident," he'd whispered, sinking down onto the edge of my bed like his legs couldn't hold him anymore. "Mom and Dad...they didn't make it home."

The way he'd held me as I screamed, as I beat my fists against his chest and demanded he take it back, demanded he tell me it was some sick joke. But Truett had never been one for jokes, especially not about something like this. He'd just held me tighter, his own tears falling into my hair as he promised me over and over that we'd be okay, that he'd take care of everything, that I'd never have to worry about anything as long as he was breathing.

And he'd kept that promise. Every single day since that night, Truett has put me first. When I wanted to go to college, he made sure it was paid for. When I came back heartbroken and lost, he never asked questions, just made space for me to heal.

He's never once made me feel like a burden, never once suggested that his life would be easier without me to worry about. Even when I know it would have been. Even when I know he could have sold the whole ranch, taken the money, and started fresh somewhere else without the weight of our parents' memory and his kid sister's dreams holding him back.

"He's going to be okay," Jesse murmurs against my ear, his voice rough with emotion. "Nora knows what she's doing. He's going to be fine."

I can hear the desperate edge to his words, the way he's trying to convince himself as much as me. Jesse and Truett have been inseparable since they were kids, getting into trouble together, working the ranch side by side, sharing dreams and disappointments, and everything in between. If something happens to Truett...

I turn in Jesse's arms, needing to see his face, needing to offer him the same comfort he's trying to give me. His green eyes are bright with unshed tears, his jaw clenched so tight I can see the muscle jumping beneath his dark beard. He looks as wrecked as I feel, and the sight of his pain somehow makes mine more bearable. We're in this together, whatever comes next.

"He's too stubborn to die," I whisper, reaching up to cup his face in my hands. The coarse hair of his beard tickles my palms, familiar and grounding. "You know how he is. He's probably already planning how to get back to work tomorrow."

Jesse's mouth quirks up in a ghost of a smile, but it doesn't reach his eyes. "Probably worried about who's going to check the north pasture fence if he's laid up."

"God knows you can't be trusted to do it right," I tease softly, and this time his smile is a little more real.

"Hey now," he protests, his voice still thick but steadier. "I've gotten better."

"Mmm," I hum noncommittally, and he huffs out a breath that might almost be a laugh under different circumstances.

We fall quiet again, watching Nora work. Her movements are sure and practiced, every gesture precise. She's completely focused on Truett, her face a mask of professional concentration, but I can see something else in the careful way she touches him, in the gentle murmur of her voice as she talks him through what she's doing, even though he's unconscious.

It hits me like a revelation, sudden and blindingly obvious now that I'm looking for it. The way Nora's eyes linger on Truett's face when she thinks no one is watching. The way her voice changes when she says his name. They may have just kissed recently, but something has been brewing for a long time.

Nora's in love with my brother.

The realization should probably surprise me more than it does, but instead it feels inevitable, like something I should have seen coming from a mile away. Nora's always been fiercely independent, never one to show her softer side to anyone. But with Truett, she's different. Gentler. More vulnerable in a way that makes my heart ache for both of them.

Does he know? I watch the way her fingers linger just a fraction too long as she checks his pulse, the way she smooths his hair back from his forehead with a tenderness that goes beyond professional care. Truett has never been great at reading emotional cues, too practical and straightforward to pick up on subtlety. He probably thinks she's just being a good friend, a good vet tech doing her job.

But the way she's looking at him now, like he's her whole world, like losing him would break something fundamental inside her...there's no mistaking it. She loves him with the kind of quiet, steady devotion that Truett deserves but has never thought to look for.

"There," Nora says finally, sitting back on her heels and surveying her work. The wound is neatly stitched, the bleeding stopped, Truett's chest rising and falling in a steady rhythm that's the most beautiful sound I've ever heard. "That should hold. Hopefully, he won't need to go to a hospital. I can only imagine the target you'll put on yourselves."

"You did good," Jesse says, his voice hoarse with gratitude. "Really good, Nora. Thank you."

She nods curtly, already starting to clean up her supplies, but I catch the way her eyes dart back to Truett's face, the way her shoulders relax just slightly now that the immediate crisis has passed.

The sound of tires on gravel announces Devlin's return, and a few minutes later, he's pushing through the door with Atlee close behind. She looks pale and shaken, her usually perfect hair disheveled, but she's clutching a small bag that might as well be treasure.

"I got everything Nora asked for," she says breathlessly, handing the bag over. "Antibiotics, pain medication, some IV fluids if you need them. I...I may have grabbed a few extra things, just in case."

"You're an angel," I tell her, meaning every word. "Both of you. I don't know how we can ever repay this."

Atlee shakes her head. "You don't need to repay anything. Just...let me know if you need more, okay? I can always go back."

Nora's already preparing a syringe, her movements quick and efficient. "This should help with the pain and get the antibiotics into his system," she explains as she finds a vein and administers the injection. "He'll probably sleep for a while, which is what he needs right now."

"Should we move him to his bed?" I ask, looking at Truett sprawled on the kitchen table. He looks too big for it, his long legs hanging off the end, and I know he'll be more comfortable in his own room.

"That's probably a good idea," Nora agrees. "But carefully. Those stitches are still fresh."

It takes all four of us, Jesse and Devlin carrying most of Truett's weight while Nora and I support his injured side, but we manage to get him to his bedroom and settled under his own covers. He stirs slightly as we move him, mumbling something incoherent that might be my name, and my heart clenches.

"Shhh," I whisper, smoothing his hair back the way our mother used to do when we were sick. "You're okay. You're home."

Nora checks his vitals one more time, adjusts his position slightly, and nods in satisfaction. "He should sleep through the night now. The fever might spike again, but that's normal. Just keep pushing fluids when he wakes up and call me if anything changes."

"You should stay," I offer, though I'm not sure where the words come from. "It's late, and you've been through hell tonight too. The guest room is made up."

For a moment, I think she's going to accept. Her eyes drift to Truett's sleeping form, and I can see the longing there, the desire to stay close and watch over him. But then she shakes her head, professional distance sliding back into place like armor.

"I should get home," she says quietly. "But I'll check on him first thing in the morning, I promise."

Devlin offers to drive her, and Atlee hugs me goodbye with promises to keep tonight's events quiet. Soon it's just Jesse and me in the suddenly too-quiet house, the adrenaline of the last few hours finally starting to wear off and leave us both shaking with exhaustion.

"Come on," Jesse says softly, taking my hand. "You need to sleep."

I want to protest, want to stay up and watch over Truett myself, but I can barely keep my eyes open. Jesse leads me to my room, but I shake my head. I want to go to the living room, where the fireplace is. "Living room. It's my comfort place. The couch with a fire blazing. It's the one thing that gets me through. Those flames licking the wood chase away all the bad thoughts and dreams."

He nods. "Let's go then." Together, we make our way downstairs, and we collapse onto the couch still fully clothed.

He pulls me against his side, and I bury my face in his chest, breathing in the familiar scent of him mixed with the lingering smell of antiseptic and fear. His heart is beating too fast under my cheek, and I know he's as wired as I am despite the bone-deep exhaustion.

"I keep thinking about what could have happened," he whispers into the darkness. "If I hadn't kept him alive on the ride home, if Nora hadn't been there..."

"But you did keep him alive on the way home," I whisper back. "And she was there. And he's going to be okay."

"I don't know what I'd do without him," Jesse admits, his voice cracking slightly. "He's...he's been my best friend since we were kids, Aubree. We've never been apart for more than a few days at a time. The thought of losing him..."

I tilt my head up to look at him, and in the dim light filtering through the curtains, I can see the tears he's trying so hard not to shed. This strong, steady man who's held me together through every crisis, who's never let me see him break, is finally showing me his own cracks.

"You're not going to lose him," I promise, pressing a soft kiss to the underside of his jaw. "We're not going to lose him. He's too stubborn, remember?"

Jesse's arms tighten around me, and I feel some of the tension leave his body. "Yeah," he breathes. "Too stubborn."

We lie there in the quiet, holding each other close, listening to the old house settle around us. Every small sound makes us both tense, straining our ears for any sign that Truett needs us, but the night stays peaceful.

Sleep comes in fits and starts, full of dreams that feel too much like memories and memories that feel too much like nightmares. I keep waking to check the clock, to listen for Truett's breathing in the next room, to make sure Jesse's still solid and warm beside me. Each time I drift off again, I'm pulled back by phantom sounds or the echo of Truett's pained groans or the sight of all that blood on my hands.

Jesse sleeps no better, his body restless against mine, his breathing uneven. Once, I wake to find him sitting on the edge of the bed, head in his hands, shoulders shaking with silent sobs. I don't say anything, just press myself against his back and wrap my arms around him until the storm passes.

When dawn finally starts to creep through the windows, painting everything in soft gray light, we're both awake, staring at the ceiling and pretending we've been sleeping.

"I should check on him," I whisper.

"Yeah," Jesse agrees, but neither of us moves for a long moment.

Finally, I force myself to get up, padding barefoot to Truett's room. He's still sleeping, but his color looks better, and when I press the back of my hand to his forehead, his temperature feels normal. The sight of his chest rising and falling steadily is the best thing I've seen in hours.

"How is he?" Jesse asks quietly from the doorway.

"Sleeping," I report, unable to keep the relief out of my voice. "No fever."

Jesse nods, some of the tension finally leaving his shoulders. "Nora'll be here soon to check on him."

"Yeah." I take one last look at my brother, at this man who's been my anchor and my protector for so many years, who last night scared me more than I've ever been scared in my life. "Jesse?"

"Yeah?"

I turn to face him, this man who's become so much more than I ever expected, who held me together when I was falling apart, who's shown me what it means to be truly, completely loved.

"Thank you," I say simply. "For everything. For being here, for...for being you."

His green eyes soften, and he crosses the room to pull me into his arms. "Where else would I be?"

Nowhere, I think as I melt against him. There's nowhere else any of us would be but right here, taking care of each other, holding each other up when the world tries to knock us down. This is what family means. Not just blood, but choice. Not just love, but commitment.

And as the morning light grows stronger, chasing away the shadows of the longest night of our lives, I know that whatever comes next, we'll face it together. All of us. Because that's what we do. That's who we are.

That's how we survive.

TWENTY
JESSE

ALL OF US are tired and mentally strung out when I head out to the barn. The hands are looking to me to figure out what needs to be done, and my brothers look like they've been up most of the night.

"Is Truett okay?" Dave asks, his eyebrows raised in concern.

"He will be. I'm not answering questions about what happened. Just know he needs some good thoughts. If you could do your normal tasks today, I'd appreciate it."

Everyone nods before leaving. Everyone, that is, except for Devlin. He glances at me, his thumbs hooked in the belt loops of his jeans. "We need to hide those trucks and trailers, Jess. I almost guarantee you that Noah will come sniffing around today. We made a lot of noise last night."

He's right. "I just can't even think straight right now. Not after what happened."

"Let me take care of this. We'll move them up to the northeast pasture, where it's almost impassable once the thaw hits. It'll hide those trucks for most of the year. By then, the heat will have died down."

I run my fingers through my hair. "Sounds like a good plan. Go on and get to it. We need to act like nothing is different around here today." Although everything is fucking different, and who knows if it'll ever be the same again. I'm heading into the office when I hear a noise at the other end of the barn, and in walks Aubree. "What are you doing here?"

She shrugs. "I couldn't stand to sit in there and wait for him to move. Cookie is checking on him when he needs it, but I had to get up and move, even if that means mucking out stalls."

"And here you say you're a city girl at heart," I reach up and move a piece of hair out of her face.

She grins, leaning in to kiss me. What's meant to be a teasing gesture turns serious real fast. Maybe because of what we've all just lived through, maybe because if I'm honest with myself, I love this girl. Who knows, but it's out of control before it even starts.

Her lips are soft against mine, but there's a desperation in the way she kisses me back that tells me she needs this as much as I do. The taste of her, sweet with just a hint of the coffee she must have grabbed from the kitchen, makes my head spin. My hands find her waist, pulling her closer until there's no space left between us.

"Jesse," she breathes against my mouth, and the way she says my name sends fire straight through my veins.

I back her up against the wooden wall of the barn, my hands tangling in that honey-blonde hair of hers. She's so damn beautiful, even with worry lines creased around those deep brown eyes. Hell, especially with them. This woman has seen us at our worst, and she's still here, still kissing me like her life depends on it.

Her fingers work at the buttons of my flannel shirt, and I let her, too caught up in the feel of her mouth on my neck to think about anything else. When her lips find that spot just below my ear, I groan, my grip tightening on her hips.

"We shouldn't be doing this here," I manage to say, even as my body argues otherwise.

"I don't care," she whispers, her breath hot against my skin. "I need to feel something other than scared right now."

I know exactly what she means. The adrenaline from last night is still coursing through me, and having her in my arms is the only thing keeping me grounded. My hands slide down to cup her ass, lifting her slightly so she can wrap her legs around my waist. The sound she makes when I press her back against the wall is enough to make me lose what's left of my control.

Her fingers trace the tattoos on my chest, and I shiver under her touch. Every nerve ending in my body is on fire, focused entirely on the places where her skin meets mine. I capture her mouth again, kissing her deeper this time, my tongue sliding against hers in a way that makes her moan into my mouth.

"God, Aubree," I breathe, pulling back just enough to look at her. Her lips are swollen from my kisses, her cheeks flushed, and that birthmark I love so much is just visible above the neckline of her shirt. "You're so fucking beautiful."

She reaches up to run her fingers through my dark hair, her nails scraping lightly against my scalp. "I love you, Jesse. I know it's crazy, but—"

I cut her off with another kiss, this one slower, more deliberate. When I pull away, I rest my forehead against hers. "It's not crazy. I love you too."

The admission hangs between us, weighted with everything we can't say out loud. That I might not be able to keep her safe. That what we did last night could tear us apart. That loving someone in this life means risking everything.

But right now, in this moment, none of that matters. All that matters is the way she feels in my arms, the way she looks at me like I'm her whole world. My hands slip under her shirt, fingers tracing the soft curve of her waist, and she arches into my touch.

"Jesse," she gasps when I find that sensitive spot just above her hip bone. Her reaction sends another wave of heat straight through me, and I press closer, letting her feel exactly what she does to me.

Her legs tighten around my waist, and I have to bite back a curse at the friction. We're playing with fire here, in broad daylight, where anyone could walk in, but I can't bring myself to stop. Not when she's making those little sounds that drive me absolutely wild.

I trail kisses down her neck, stopping to pay special attention to the spot where her pulse is racing. She tastes like sunshine and something uniquely her, and I want to memorize every inch of her skin with my mouth. When I reach the collar of her shirt, I push it aside, revealing more of that creamy skin I've been dreaming about.

"We need to stop," I murmur against her throat, even as my hands continue their exploration of her curves.

"Do we?" she asks, her voice breathy and full of want. Her fingers find the buckle of my belt, and I nearly lose it right there.

"Aubree..."

The sound of tires on gravel cuts through the haze of desire like a bucket of cold water. We freeze, listening as a truck door slams somewhere outside the barn.

"Shit," I breathe, carefully setting her back on her feet. She smooths down her shirt while I button my flannel, both of us trying to look like we weren't just seconds away from tearing each other's clothes off.

Heavy footsteps echo through the barn, and I recognize the deliberate cadence before Noah even comes into view. He's wearing his sheriff's uniform, hat pulled low over his eyes, and the expression on his face tells me this isn't a social visit.

"Morning, Jesse," he says, tipping his hat to Aubree. "Miss Aubree."

"Noah." I nod, hoping my voice sounds steadier than I feel. "What brings you out here so early?"

He hooks his thumbs in his belt, a gesture that makes the gun on his hip more prominent. "Had some reports of cattle rustling last night. Trucks and trailers moving around late. You wouldn't know anything about that, would you?"

I keep my expression neutral, even as my heart pounds against my ribs. "Can't say I do. We were all pretty beat after the day we had yesterday."

"That's right, I heard Truett got hurt. How's he doing?"

The way he phrases it, like he already knows the answer, makes my skin crawl. But I keep my voice level. "He'll be fine. You know how it is. There's a danger being out this far and working the way we do."

Noah's eyes narrow slightly, and I can practically see the wheels turning in his head. He's good at his job. I'll give him that. Too good sometimes.

"Funny thing," he continues, taking a step closer. "I had three different calls about trucks heading this direction around midnight. Kinda like y'all's trucks, from the sound of it. Said they saw cattle on them."

I shrug, fighting to keep my breathing even. "Sounds like a good night for whoever those cattle belonged to."

"Mmm." Noah's gaze flicks to Aubree, then back to me. "You mind if I take a look around? Just to be thorough."

Every instinct I have screams at me to say no, but that would be as good as an admission of guilt. Instead, I gesture toward the barn. "Help yourself. Though I'm not sure what you're expecting to find."

He starts walking through the barn, his trained eyes taking in every detail. I watch him carefully, knowing that any sign of nervousness could give us away. Beside me, Aubree has gone perfectly still, and I can feel the tension radiating off her in waves.

Noah stops at one of the empty stalls, running his hand along the wood. "This one looks like it's been cleaned recently."

"We clean all the stalls regularly," I say. "Part of running a proper operation."

"Of course." He continues his inspection, checking corners and shadows like he's looking for something specific. When he reaches the far end of the barn, he pauses at the large doors that lead to the back pastures.

"Those tire tracks out there look pretty fresh," he observes.

"Feed truck was here yesterday afternoon," I lie smoothly. "Had to back all the way up to get the hay unloaded. When she was in town the other day"—I nod to Aubree—"she only got part of our order."

Noah turns back to face me, and there's something in his expression that makes my blood run cold. He knows. Maybe he can't prove it yet, but he knows we were involved in whatever went down last night.

"You know, Jesse, I've been a sheriff's deputy in this county for going on five years now. In that time, I've learned to trust my instincts. And right now, they're telling me that you and your brothers might want to stay close to town for the next few days."

The warning is clear, even if he's couching it in friendly terms. "And why would we want to do that?"

"Oh, just in case there are questions that need answering. Questions that folks might not be prepared for if they're caught off guard." His smile doesn't reach his eyes. "You understand."

I meet his gaze steadily, calling on every ounce of control I possess. "Can't imagine what questions those would be, Noah. We're not hiding anything here."

"I'm sure you're not," he says, but the tone suggests otherwise. "Still, might be smart to keep your schedule flexible. You never know when duty might call."

He tips his hat again to Aubree, who has remained silent through the entire exchange. "Miss Aubree, always a pleasure. Take care of yourself."

With that, he turns and walks back toward the front of the barn, his footsteps echoing in the sudden silence. I wait until I hear his truck start and pull away before I allow myself to breathe again.

"Fuck," I mutter, running both hands through my hair. "That was too close."

Aubree moves to my side, her face pale. "He knows, doesn't he?"

"He suspects. There's a difference, but not much of one." I pull her against me, needing to feel her warmth to counteract the cold dread spreading through my chest. "We need to be careful. More careful than we've ever been."

"What does this mean for us? For Truett?"

I wish I had a good answer for her, but the truth is, I don't know. Noah Sanchez is like a dog with a bone when he gets his teeth into something, and he's clearly gotten his teeth into this. The fact that he knows about Truett's injury means someone saw something, and that's never a good sign.

"It means we stick to our story, and we don't give him any reason to dig deeper," I say, trying to sound more confident than I feel. "As long as we're smart about this, we'll be fine."

But even as I say the words, I'm not sure I believe them. The way Noah looked at me, the careful phrasing of his warning, it all points to trouble ahead. Big trouble.

I think about the trucks and trailers that Devlin is hopefully moving to the northeast pasture right now. About the evidence that might still be scattered around the property. About Truett, lying unconscious in the house, unable to back up whatever story we decide to tell.

"Jesse?" Aubree's voice pulls me out of my spiraling thoughts. "You're scaring me."

I look down at her, at the worry written across her beautiful face, and I make a decision. Whatever happens next, I'm going to protect her, even if it means sacrificing everything else.

"Come here," I say, pulling her fully into my arms. She melts against me, and for a moment, the fear recedes. "We're going to get through this. All of us."

"Promise me," she whispers against my chest.

"I promise," I say, and I mean it, even if I have no idea how I'm going to keep that promise.

The sound of another truck approaching makes us both tense, but it's just Devlin returning from his trip to the northeast pasture. His face is grim as he walks into the barn.

"Noah was just here," I tell him before he can speak.

"Shit. What did he want?"

"To let us know that he's watching. And to suggest that we might want to stay close to town in case there are questions."

Devlin's jaw tightens. "Questions about what?"

"About three trailers that someone saw with cattle on them late last night," I say. "About those trucks and trailers moving around in the middle of the night. About Truett's convenient accident."

"How much does he know?"

"Enough to be dangerous. Not enough to arrest us. Yet."

We stand there in silence for a moment, the weight of our situation settling over us like a heavy blanket. Everything we've worked for, everything we've built, could come crashing down around us. And there's not a damn thing we can do about it except wait and see what Noah's next move will be.

"What do we do now?" Aubree asks quietly.

I look at my brother, then at the woman I love, and I feel the familiar weight of responsibility settling on my shoulders. It's up to me to figure this out, to find a way to protect my family and the ranch that's been in our blood for generations.

"Now we act normal," I say finally. "We take care of Truett, we run the ranch, and we don't give Noah Sanchez any reason to think we're anything other than what we appear to be."

But even as I say it, I know it's going to be harder than it sounds. Because Noah isn't going to let this go. He's going to keep digging until he finds what he's looking for, and when he does, we're all going to pay the price.

The question is: will we be ready for him when that time comes?

As Aubree slips her hand into mine, her fingers intertwining with mine, I realize that ready or not, we're about to find out. And this time, there might not be a way out of the situation we've gotten ourselves into.

The ranch has always been worth fighting for. Now I just hope it won't cost us everything to keep it.

TWENTY-ONE
NORA

I PULL into the driveway of the Grizzly River Ranch and slowly take the gravel road down to the big house. I should be at work, but I called in because I can't concentrate knowing that Truett is injured.

Leaving him last night was one of the hardest things I've ever done. I've loved him since I was a teenager, and he was just my best friend's older brother. I've sat back and watched as he's done what he's had to do in order to keep their ranch afloat.

I've listened to him worry about when Aubree was living in Chicago.

I've seen him date other women.

But through it all, my stupid heart has clenched every single time I've gotten a glimpse of him in a crowd.

Parking my truck, I get out and then take the steps quickly, before knocking on the door. Cookie answers, a smile on his face.

"Hey girl, come on in. Heard you saved our boy last night."

My cheeks heat with embarrassment. I hate being the center

of attention. "Yeah, can't take much credit because he did most of it himself. I'm just glad I gave him a fighting chance."

"That you did."

"Has he been awake yet today?" I ask, following him to the kitchen.

"Off and on, here and there. I've been keeping up with his pain medication, but it's almost time for it again, so he might be more lucid."

"Good, I'm going to go check on him."

I've been in this house more times than I care to count, but today it feels so much different than it ever has before.

Walking down the familiar hallway toward Truett's room, my heart pounds against my ribs like a caged bird. The floorboards creak under my boots, the same sounds I've heard a thousand times growing up here visiting Aubree, but now each step feels weighted with something I can't name. Fear? Hope? Both?

I pause outside his door, my hand hovering over the handle. Through the thin wood, I can hear the soft sound of his breathing, steady and strong. Relief floods through me so completely that I have to lean against the doorframe for support.

Taking a deep breath, I turn the handle and step inside.

The room is dim, curtains drawn against the afternoon sun, but there's enough light filtering through to see him clearly. Truett lies propped up against a mountain of pillows, his chest bare except for the white bandages wrapped around his torso. Dark stubble covers his jaw, making the sharp angles of his face even more pronounced. Even injured, even pale, he's the most beautiful thing I've ever seen.

His eyes are closed, thick lashes casting shadows on his

cheekbones, and for a moment, I just stand there, drinking him in. Alive. Safe. Here.

"You gonna stand there all day staring at me, or are you gonna come closer?"

His voice, rough with sleep and medication, makes me jump. Those storm-gray eyes are open now, watching me with an intensity that makes my cheeks burn.

"I wasn't staring," I lie, crossing the room to the chair beside his bed. "I was just...checking to make sure you were still breathing."

A slow smile spreads across his lips. "Still breathing, thanks to you."

I settle into the chair, suddenly nervous. "Cookie said you've been in and out all day. How are you feeling?"

"Like I got trampled by a bull and then shot," he says with a dry laugh that turns into a wince. "But alive, which I hear I owe to you."

"You don't owe me anything, Truett. Anyone would have done the same thing."

His expression grows serious, those gray eyes searching my face. "No, Nora. Not anyone. You saved my life. Cookie told me what you did. You saved my life."

The weight in his voice, the raw gratitude, makes my throat tight. "I just did what needed to be done. You would have done the same for me."

"In a heartbeat," he says without hesitation. "But that doesn't make what you did any less incredible. Thank you, Nora. For everything. For being there when I needed you most."

Tears prick at my eyes, and I have to look away before they spill over. "You don't have to thank me. I couldn't...I can't imagine..." My voice breaks, and I take a shaky breath. "I don't know what I would do if anything happened to you. If something took you away from me permanently."

The admission hangs between us, raw and honest. I've never said anything so vulnerable to him before, never let him see how deeply my feelings run. But last night changed everything. Coming so close to losing him stripped away all my carefully constructed walls.

When I finally look back at him, his expression has shifted to something I've never seen before, soft and wondering, like he's seeing me for the first time.

"Nora," he says quietly, and my name on his lips sounds different somehow. Like a prayer, or a promise. "You have no idea how long I've wanted to hear you say something like that."

My heart stutters. "What do you mean?"

He's quiet for a long moment, his eyes never leaving mine. When he speaks, his voice is barely above a whisper. "I mean, I feel the same way. The thought of something happening to you, of losing you...it would destroy me. You've been the one constant good thing in my life, even when I was too stupid to see it clearly."

Hope blooms in my chest, wild and desperate. "Truett..."

But he holds up a hand, stopping me. Pain flickers across his features, not physical pain, but something deeper. "But I can't. Not yet. Not until I'm worthy of you."

"What are you talking about? You're already..."

"No, I'm not." His voice is firm, final. "Look at me, Nora. Really look. I'm lying here shot because I got mixed up in something dangerous. I've been making questionable choices trying to keep this ranch afloat, putting myself and everyone I care about at risk. You deserve better than that. You deserve someone who can protect you, not someone who brings danger to your door."

Frustration flares in my chest. "That's not your decision to make. You don't get to decide what I deserve or what I can handle."

"Don't I?" His jaw tightens. "When it's your safety on the line? When it's your life that could be in danger because of my choices?"

I want to argue, want to tell him he's being ridiculous, but movement outside the window catches my eye. A familiar truck is pulling up the drive. Noah's patrol vehicle. My stomach sinks.

"Truett," I say quietly, nodding toward the window. "Noah's here. He's talking to Jesse and Aubree."

Truett turns his head to look, his expression darkening. Even from here, we can see the serious set of Noah's shoulders, the way Jesse's hands clench into fists at his sides, the worried look on Aubree's face.

"Shit," Truett mutters, trying to push himself up straighter. The movement makes him grimace, and I automatically reach out to steady him.

"Don't," I warn. "You'll tear your stitches."

He settles back against the pillows, but his whole body is tense. "They probably want to question us about last night. Someone probably told them the trucks and trailers headed toward the ranch."

"What were you doing last night?" I ask, though part of me isn't sure I want to know.

His laugh is bitter. "Something stupid. Something I thought would help save the ranch, but instead nearly got me killed." He looks at me then, his expression pained. "This is exactly what

I'm talking about, Nora. This is why I need to stay away from you until I get my life straightened out."

"Stay away from me?" The words hit like a physical blow. "You're going to shut me out because of this?"

"I have to. I won't put you in danger. I won't risk—"

"Stop." My voice is sharper than I intended, cutting through his words. I stand up, pacing to the window where I can see Noah gesturing toward the house. "Just stop talking like you have all the control here."

"Nora..."

I whirl around to face him. "No, Truett. You listen to me. You just told me you've wanted to hear me say how I feel about you. Well, here's some more honesty for you. I'm tired of you making decisions for me like I'm some fragile flower who can't handle the truth or make her own choices."

His eyes widen, but I'm not done.

"Do you think I don't know what you've been doing to try to save this ranch? I've lived in this community my entire life. I'm not blind, Truett. And I'm not stupid."

"I never said you were."

"But you're treating me like I am." I move closer to the bed, my hands clenched into fists. "You're sitting there talking about staying away from me 'for my own good' like I don't get a say in it. Like my feelings don't matter. Like I'm not strong enough to handle whatever comes next."

He stares at me, something like awe flickering in his expression. "Nora..."

"I've been in love with you since I was seventeen years old," I continue, the words pouring out of me like water through a broken dam. "Seventeen, Truett. That's eight years of watching you from the sidelines, eight years of hoping you'd see me as more than just Aubree's best friend. Eight years of keeping my mouth shut while you dated other women and made decisions that broke my heart."

Tears are streaming down my face now, but I don't care. I'm past caring about anything except making him understand.

"So don't you dare sit there and tell me what I can and can't handle. Don't you dare try to protect me from the choices I want to make. If I want to be with you, danger and all, that's my choice. Not yours."

The room falls silent except for the sound of our breathing. Truett's eyes never leave my face, and I can see a war playing out behind them—want and fear, hope and desperation.

Outside, I hear Noah's truck door slam, footsteps on the gravel. He'll be at the door any minute.

"Eight years," Truett says finally, his voice hoarse.

"Eight years," I confirm.

"And you never said anything."

"Neither did you."

He closes his eyes, leaning his head back against the pillows. "God, Nora. I don't deserve you."

Despite everything, I laugh. It's watery and shaky, but it's real. "Yes, you do."

When he opens his eyes again, they're burning with an intensity that makes my knees weak. "If I kiss you right now, there's no going back. No matter what happens with Noah, with the ranch, with whatever mess I've gotten myself into, if I kiss you, I'm not letting you go again."

My heart pounds so hard I'm sure he can hear it. "Good," I whisper. "Because I'm not going anywhere."

He reaches for me then, his hand cupping the back of my neck, pulling me down until our foreheads touch. "I want you," he breathes against my lips. "I've wanted you for so damn long I can't remember what it felt like before."

"I want you too," I whisper back.

And then he's kissing me, soft and desperate and full of eight years of waiting. His lips are warm and sure against mine, his hand tangling in my hair. The kiss tastes like promises and hope and coming home.

When we break apart, I'm breathless. He's looking at me like I'm something miraculous, something he can't quite believe is real.

"We'll figure it out," I tell him, my voice stronger now. "Whatever trouble you're in, whatever's coming next, we'll figure it out together."

He nods, his thumb stroking across my cheek. "Together."

Truett's hand finds mine, our fingers interlacing. His grip is strong and sure, an anchor in whatever storm is about to break over us.

"With you? I'm ready for anything."

TWENTY-TWO
AUBREE

"ARE you taking the cattle to market tomorrow?" I ask Jesse as we sit on the couch in front of the fireplace a few days later.

At some point, it'll get too warm to have the fire going, but right now it offers me some comfort in these uncertain times.

"Yeah, and I'm sending you to Nora's. I don't want you out here while we're gone."

I tilt my gaze up to him. "What about Truett?"

"He'll be well taken care of. You, Atlee, and Nora will be together at Nora's. The three of you are the ones I'm most concerned about."

This is different for us. I've never known him to worry about anyone other than his brothers or Truett. He's never been the type of person to show his feelings. The I love you he gave me was a crack in the armor, and I don't expect it to show up very often. "What do you think's going to happen?"

"You never know. The men at the Morrison place probably saw that it was us. Do I know that for sure? No. It was dark, and there was a lot going on, but I know that Noah suspects more than he's letting on. My fear is he'll catch y'all at a vulnerable time and someone will slip up." He frames my face with his hands. "I'm not going to let that happen."

There he is. The man who's harder than he needs to be. The one who can strike a tiny sliver of fear into anyone with a few words and a stern look.

"We wouldn't betray you."

His palm moves to the back of my head, and he cups it surprisingly softly. "I'm not saying you would, but any of you could be used against us. I'm not willing to put you in that situation."

Warmth creeps into my chest, whether it should or not. Knowing that he cares enough about me that I could be used against him is flattering. It gives me hope that this isn't just some fling, and he's praying I'll leave again.

"What's going on in that head of yours?" His deep voice is laced with a grin. "I can hear it contemplating."

I smile at him before rolling us over so that I'm straddling his waist. He slaps his hands onto my hips, holding me close. "Just eighteen-year-old me is really excited she's in this position."

He presses up into me. "Well, thirty-something-year-old me is happy about it too."

The firelight dances across his face, highlighting the sharp angles of his jaw and the intensity in those striking green eyes. My fingers trace the dark beard that frames his mouth, feeling the coarse hair beneath my fingertips. He's beautiful in that rugged, dangerous way that's always made my pulse quicken.

"You know what I was thinking about earlier?" I murmur,

my hands sliding down to rest on his chest, feeling the steady thrum of his heartbeat beneath my palms.

"Tell me," he says, his voice rough with desire as his thumbs trace circles on my hip bones.

"I keep thinking about what would have happened if I hadn't gotten embarrassed and left after I kissed you." I lean down, my honey-blonde hair falling like a curtain around us. "What if I would've been brave enough to stay?"

His hands slide up my sides, leaving trails of fire in their wake. "Maybe we needed those years apart. Maybe we both had some growing up to do."

"Maybe," I whisper against his lips before capturing them in a kiss that starts soft but quickly deepens. He tastes like whiskey and promises, like everything I've ever wanted but was too scared to reach for.

His hands find the hem of my shirt, and I help him pull it over my head, the fabric joining the growing pile on the floor. The firelight plays across my skin, and I watch as his gaze traces the heart-shaped birthmark on my breast, his finger following the same path.

"Perfect," he murmurs, his voice thick with reverence that makes my chest tight with emotion.

I reach for the buttons of his shirt, my fingers working with practiced ease now. Each inch of revealed skin shows more of the tattoos that tell the story of his life. Some I recognize from before. Others are new, marking the years we spent apart.

"This one's new," I say, tracing a particularly intricate design that wraps around his ribs.

"Got it about two years after you left," he admits, his breath hitching as my fingers explore the ink. "Needed something to focus on besides wishing I would've responded to that kiss."

The admission catches me off guard, raw and honest in a way that Jesse rarely allows himself to be. I lean down and press my lips to the tattoo, tasting salt and skin and something uniquely him.

His hands are everywhere now, relearning the curves of my body with a reverence that speaks louder than any words he could say. When he rolls us over, positioning himself above me. The firelight catches in his dark hair, and I think I've never seen anything more beautiful than this man who's claimed my heart twice now.

"Aubree," he breathes my name like a prayer, and I arch up to meet him, our bodies fitting together like they were made for this, for each other.

The world narrows to just us—the crackle of the fire, the sound of our breathing, the whispered words of need and want that fall from our lips. He moves with a controlled intensity that sets my nerves on fire, each touch deliberate and claiming.

When I wrap my legs around his waist, pulling him deeper, he groans against my neck, his beard rough against my sensitive skin. "God, Aubree. You're going to be the death of me."

"Good way to go," I manage to gasp out, my nails digging into the muscles of his back as he finds that perfect rhythm that makes my entire world tilt on its axis.

He lifts his head to look at me, those green eyes dark with desire and something deeper, more dangerous. "Look at me," he commands, and I do, even as my body threatens to fall apart beneath his touch. "I need to see you."

So I keep my eyes locked on his as he takes us both over the edge, as my name falls from his lips like a benediction and his fills my throat in a cry that echoes off the cabin walls.

Afterward, we lay tangled together on the couch, my head on his chest, listening to his heartbeat slowly return to normal. His fingers curl through my hair, and I trace lazy patterns on his skin, both of us reluctant to break the spell of intimacy that surrounds us.

"Jesse," I finally whisper, my voice still hoarse.

"Mmm?" The sound rumbles through his chest.

"Be careful tomorrow. Please." I lift my head to look at him, suddenly struck by how dangerous his world really is, how easily I could lose him again. "I know you can take care of yourself, but..."

He cups my face, his thumb brushing over my lower lip. "Hey. I'm not going anywhere, darlin'. Not again."

"Promise me."

"I promise," he says, and there's something in his voice that makes me believe him completely. "But you be careful too. Stay with Nora and Atlee. Don't take any risks."

I nod, though part of me chafes at being protected, at being seen as something that needs guarding. But I understand now that it's not about my capabilities. It's about how much I mean to him, how the thought of losing me terrifies him as much as losing him terrifies me.

"Jesse?" I trace the line of his collarbone, gathering my courage. "I need you to know something."

He goes still beneath me, his hand pausing in my hair. "What?"

"I care about you. So much more than I should, probably. More than is smart or safe or logical." The words tumble out in a rush, years of bottled-up feelings finally finding their voice. "I know we're complicated, and I know your world is dangerous, but I—"

He silences me with a kiss, soft and lingering and full of things he's not ready to say out loud yet. When he pulls back, his eyes are soft in a way I rarely get to see.

"You think I don't feel the same?" His voice is rough with emotion. "You think I'd be sending you away tomorrow if you didn't mean everything to me?"

My heart stutters in my chest. "Everything?"

"Everything," he confirms, his hand sliding down to rest over my heart. "You scared the hell out of me when you came back. I'd finally gotten to a place where I could function without the thought of those lips against mine, and then there you were, and I realized I'd just been going through the motions."

I press my palm over his hand, holding it against my chest where my heart is beating so hard I'm sure he can feel it. "I love you," I whisper, the words slipping out before I can stop them. We've said them before, but it was in an emotionally higher situation.

His sharp intake of breath tells me he heard them, and for a moment, panic flickers through me. Too much, too soon, too...

"I love you too," he says quietly, and the world stops spinning for a heartbeat before it starts up again, faster and more vivid than before. "God help us both, but I love you too."

Relief floods through me, followed immediately by a terror so acute it steals my breath. Loving Jesse has always been dangerous. He's the kind of man who burns bright and lives hard, who makes enemies as easily as he makes allies. But lying here in his arms, watching the firelight play across his features, I know I'd rather have this, as dangerous and uncertain as it is, than spend another day pretending I could be happy without him.

"We're a mess," I murmur against his chest, pressing a kiss to his heart.

"Yeah," he agrees, his arms tightening around me. "But we're our mess."

The fire begins to die down, casting longer shadows across the room, but neither of us moves to tend it. Tomorrow will bring cattle runs and separations and all the dangers that come with the life Jesse's chosen. But tonight, we have this—the warmth of the dying fire, the solid reality of each other's bodies, and the fragile, fierce thing that's grown between us.

"Get some sleep," he murmurs against my hair. "Tomorrow's going to be a long day."

I nestle closer, breathing in his scent—leather and smoke and something wild that's purely Jesse. "Are you going to drop me off at Nora's?"

"Yeah, darlin'. I'll drop you off."

His breathing evens out beneath me, but I stay awake a while longer, memorizing the feeling of his arms around me, the sound of his heartbeat, the way his chest rises and falls with each breath. In a few hours, he'll be gone, and I'll be left with Nora and Atlee, waiting and worrying and trying not to think about all the things that could go wrong.

But right now, in this moment stolen from time, everything is perfect. And maybe that's enough. Maybe these perfect moments are what make all the danger and uncertainty worth it.

The fire crackles one last time before settling into embers, and I finally let sleep take me, safe in the arms of the man who's always been my greatest risk and my deepest desire.

TWENTY-THREE
JESSE

"WHO'S WATCHING US?" Aubree asks as I pull up to the curb in front of Nora's apartment.

"You don't have to worry about that. All you have to worry about is staying safe while I'm gone. Devlin and I will be here to pick you up after the sale."

"Good, then you can take us all out for dinner. We've only ever been to the bar, Jesse. I'd like to be seen on your arm in this town, if at all possible."

My heart stutters in my chest. "Are you sure? You wanna be seen with me?"

"Why wouldn't I? You've selflessly made sure my brother's ranch has stayed afloat for the last eight years, while sacrificing what you could've done for yourself, regardless of how y'all did it and what you've had to do. You're a good man."

She doesn't know the half of it. "I'm not a good man, and I'm not selfless. Your ranch has put food on the table for my entire family and made sure we had a roof over our heads. I'm grateful."

"Then be grateful by taking me out for dinner. Please?"

"I'm going to have Devlin with me," I argue. Dinner is not my type of schtick.

"He can come too. I'm sure he owes Atlee a good time. No telling how gruff he was, ordering her around the night my brother got shot."

I grin, just imagining it. There's a ten-year age gap between the two of them, and my brother has never been accused of being soft about anything. "Fuck, okay. We'll be here. But you have to promise not to go outside until we come and get you."

She seems to contemplate what I've said, but in the end, she leans in, placing a kiss on my cheek. "I promise we won't open the door for anyone except you."

"Good, I just want you to stay safe. Do I need to walk you up there?"

She shakes her head. "Nora's standing right there. I think we'll be fine."

With another kiss, she's out the door and heading up the stairs with Nora. They both wave at me, and then I'm off to the market. Devlin's meeting me there with a semi full of cattle, and when we're done, hopefully we can put this whole situation behind us.

The livestock market sits on the outskirts of Grizzly River. I can smell the dust and manure before I even turn into the gravel lot, the familiar scent mixing with diesel fumes from the idling trucks. My hands tighten on the steering wheel as I scan the area, looking for any sign of the Morrison boys or their associates.

Devlin's already there when I arrive, his massive frame leaning against the side of our cattle trailer. Even from a distance, I can see the tension in his shoulders, the way his dark eyes sweep the lot. Eight years in the Army before he came back to help run the ranch left their mark on him. He's always been the more cautious one between us.

"See anything?" I ask as I approach, my boots crunching on the gravel.

"Couple of Morrison's hired hands by the loading dock," he says, nodding toward the far end of the market. "But no sign of the brothers themselves."

I follow his gaze and spot them, two men in worn jeans and dirty caps, leaning against a pickup truck. They're trying to look casual, but their eyes keep drifting our way.

"They're keeping tabs," I mutter.

"'Course they are. Question is whether they're here to start trouble or just gather intel."

Carson pulls up, riding with a friend from a neighboring ranch, so that he can drive the cattle trailer home, and Devlin can head back into town with me.

The next few hours pass in a blur of adrenaline and forced normalcy. We move through the familiar rhythm of the cattle sale—inspecting our animals one final time, registering with the auctioneer, then watching from the bleachers as lot after lot goes through the ring.

Devlin stays close, his presence a comforting weight beside me. We've done this dance so many times over the years, but today feels different. The stakes are higher now, with Truett laid up and Aubree's future hanging in the balance.

When our first lot enters the ring, I hold my breath. Twenty-five head of prime Angus steers, their black coats gleaming under the auction house lights. The bidding starts strong and climbs steadily, buyers recognizing quality when they see it.

"Sold for twelve hundred per head," the auctioneer's voice booms through the speakers.

Devlin lets out a low whistle. "Damn good price."

Our second lot does even better, thirty head of heifers that bring in thirteen-fifty each. By the time our final group goes through, I'm starting to believe we might actually pull this off without incident.

The Morrison hands stay put throughout the entire sale, watching but not interfering. Maybe they're smarter than I gave them credit for. Starting trouble at a public cattle auction would draw too much attention, even for them.

When the last of our cattle sells for another strong price, I feel some of the tension leave my shoulders. We've done it. The ranch has enough money to stay afloat for another season, maybe two if we're careful.

Carson meets us at the settlement office. "Ready when you are."

I take the check from the clerk, the paper feeling heavier than it should in my hands. This represents all the danger we've put ourselves into in order to make a living.

"Take it back with ya. We'll be home sometime tonight." I hand him the check and watch as he runs off with a grin on his face.

Devlin and I walk back to my truck in comfortable silence, both of us keeping an eye on our surroundings. The Morrison hands are nowhere to be seen now. Hopefully, they didn't see anything that made them suspicious.

"Think they'll make a move?" Devlin asks as we climb into the cab.

"Not yet. They can't pin it on anyone, at least not yet." I start the engine and pull out of the lot, taking the long way back toward town. "Hopefully, they let it go. They can't get them back now, anyway."

The drive back to Nora's apartment takes longer than it should, partly because I'm being extra careful about checking for tails, and partly because I'm nervous as hell about this dinner. Taking Aubree out in public feels like crossing a line somehow—making our relationship official in a way that can't be taken back.

Not that I want to take it back. The woman has gotten under my skin in ways I never expected, and the thought of her leaving for Chicago makes my chest tight with something I don't want to name.

Nora's apartment building comes into view. I texted her to let her know we were close, and as Aubree comes down the stairs, I can see she's changed into a dress that hugs her curves in all the right places, her honey-blonde hair catching the late afternoon sun. Even from here, I can see the nervous energy in her posture.

Atlee stands beside her in jeans and a fitted top, looking like she'd rather be anywhere else. She's younger than we are, and no doubt she feels a little out of place.

"About time," Devlin mutters, but I catch the way his eyes linger on Atlee as we pull up to the curb.

The women approach the truck, and I'm struck again by

how beautiful Aubree looks. The dress brings out the warm brown of her eyes, and when she smiles at me through the passenger window, I feel that familiar kick in my chest.

"How did it go?" she asks as she climbs into the front seat.

"Better than expected," I reply, starting the engine as Atlee and Devlin settle into the back. "We're officially in the black for the rest of the year."

"I'm so glad!" Aubree's genuine excitement makes something warm unfurl in my chest. "I knew you could do it."

"We all did it," I correct, glancing at her sideways. "It's a team effort."

"Speaking of teams," Atlee pipes up from the back seat, "Nora's heading out to the ranch to check on Truett and bring him some dinner. She said to tell y'all have fun and not hurry back since she'll be there."

There's something in her tone that makes me glance in the rearview mirror. Atlee's looking out the window, but I catch the slight flush in her cheeks. Interesting.

"Where are we going for this fancy dinner?" Devlin asks, and I can hear the reluctance in his voice.

"The Cattleman's Inn," Aubree says before I can answer. "It's in Millfield, about twenty minutes from here. I looked it up online. They have excellent steaks and a nice atmosphere."

Millfield. One town over, where we're less likely to run into anyone we know. Smart thinking.

The drive passes pleasantly, with Aubree and Atlee chatting about everything from the ranch to Aubree's life in Chicago. I find myself relaxing as we put distance between us and the day's tensions, letting the familiar rhythm of the road soothe my nerves.

The Cattleman's Inn turns out to be exactly what Aubree promised, a rustic but upscale steakhouse with warm lighting and comfortable booths. The hostess seats us at a corner table with a good view of the dining room, and I make a mental note of the exits out of habit.

"This is nice," Aubree says, settling beside me in the booth. Her leg brushes against mine under the table, and I have to fight the urge to pull her closer.

"Better than the Rusty Spur," Atlee admits, studying her menu. "Though their burgers are pretty good."

Devlin snorts. "Everything's better than the Rusty Spur. That place is held together by duct tape and stubbornness."

We order drinks—beer for Devlin and me, wine for the women—and settle into easy conversation. For the first time in weeks, I allow myself to relax completely, enjoying the simple pleasure of good company and the promise of a decent meal.

"So," Atlee says after the waitress brings our drinks. "What's the plan now? I mean, with the sale done and Truett on the mend."

The question I've been dreading. I steal a glance at Aubree, trying to read her expression in the dim light.

"Well," Aubree says slowly, swirling her wine glass. "I suppose that depends on a lot of things."

"Such as?" I ask, though I'm not sure I want to hear the answer.

She meets my eyes, and I see something complicated there—want and uncertainty warring in her brown gaze. "Such as whether there's a reason for me to stay."

The words hang in the air between us, heavy with implication. Across the table, Devlin and Atlee exchange a look that's equal parts knowing and uncomfortable.

"Chicago's got opportunities," Atlee says carefully. "Your job, your life there."

I wonder what they talked about while they were at Nora's apartment all day.

"Chicago's also got concrete and noise and people who don't know the first thing about what matters," Aubree replies. "Sometimes opportunities aren't worth much if you're not happy."

My heart starts beating faster, but I force myself to stay calm. "And are you? Happy, I mean. Here."

She reaches under the table and finds my hand, her fingers interlacing with mine. "Getting there."

The food arrives before I can respond, giving us all something to focus on besides the elephant in the room. The steaks are perfectly cooked, the sides abundant, and the conversation flows more easily once we're eating.

Devlin tells stories about his Army days that have Atlee laughing despite herself. Aubree shares memories of growing up on the ranch before her parents died, painting pictures of a childhood I can barely imagine. For a couple of hours, we're just four people enjoying a good meal and each other's company.

It's almost enough to make me forget about the Morrison brothers, about Truett's shooting, about all the complications that brought us to this point. Almost.

"This was perfect," Aubree says as we finish dessert, leaning into my side with contentment. "Thank you for agreeing to come."

"Thank you for talking me into it," I reply, and I mean it. This—sitting here with her, watching Devlin slowly warm up to the idea of actually enjoying himself, seeing Atlee smile more than she has in months—this feels like something worth fighting for.

We're getting ready to leave, Devlin arguing good-naturedly with the waitress about who's paying the check, when I spot a familiar figure near the hostess station. My blood turns cold as Noah Sanchez turns around, his eyes scanning the dining room until they land on our table.

"Shit," I mutter under my breath.

"What?" Aubree follows my gaze and stiffens. "Oh."

Noah approaches our table with that easy, practiced smile that doesn't reach his eyes. He's out of uniform but still carries himself like law enforcement, all confident swagger and barely concealed suspicion.

"Well, well," he says, stopping beside our booth. "Fancy meeting y'all here. Having a celebration?"

"Just dinner," I reply carefully, my hand finding Aubree's under the table. "Didn't expect to see you in Millfield."

"Funny thing about that," Noah says, his smile never wavering. "I'm still working on those alibis from the night Truett was hurt. You know how it is...crossing t's and dotting i's."

The temperature at our table drops about ten degrees. Devlin's gone perfectly still, and I can feel Atlee's tension from across the booth.

"Speaking of which," Noah continues, turning his attention to Aubree. "I don't think I ever got a clear answer about where Jesse was that night. Mind helping me out with that?"

The question hangs in the air like a loaded gun. I can feel my pulse hammering in my throat, waiting to see what Aubree will say. We never discussed this, never coordinated our stories. Hell,

I'm not even sure she knows the full extent of what happened that night.

But when she looks up at Noah, her brown eyes are clear and steady, her voice calm and certain.

"He was with me," she says without a second's hesitation.

My heart does a jump and a twirl, because that means without a doubt, that she's staying.

TWENTY-FOUR
AUBREE

I WATCH Jesse drive away from Nora's apartment, heading to take the cattle to market. I've never worried about him leaving before, but now I do. Since Truett got shot, I've worried about a lot more than I ever have before.

Nora opens the door with a smile before I can even knock. Atlee is sitting on her couch, and it looks like Nora was sitting across from her.

"Welcome to our prison." Atlee rolls her eyes, blowing a breath. "No one's ever told me I'm not allowed to leave somewhere before, and I'm not sure I like the implication that Devlin Nelson is in charge of me."

Nora and I glance at each other.

"So you're saying it doesn't turn you on just a little bit that he laid down the law to you?"

Atlee shifts in her seat. "I wouldn't know. I've never had a man act like that before, but it was interesting."

Nora brings coffee to the table. "My question is, what was he like on your drive to the ranch the night that Truett was shot. Devlin hardly ever says five words."

Atlee's face pinkens. "He spoke. Not a lot, but he was nice to me."

"Atlee..." I give her a grin. "Did the strong, silent type do it for you?"

"There was something about the way he grunted every answer to any question I had that did seem pretty hot."

We both giggle at her. "Welcome to the club, honey. All of 'em grunt every answer to any question asked."

The laughter feels good, a brief respite from the tension that's been hanging over all of us like a storm cloud. I curl my legs under me on Nora's plush armchair, wrapping my hands around the warm coffee mug. The apartment smells like vanilla and cinnamon, so different from the hay and leather scents I've grown accustomed to at the ranch.

"Speaking of grunting men," Nora says, settling back into her spot across from Atlee. "How is Truett really doing, Aubree? I know when I visit him at the ranch, he puts on this tough act, but I can see right through it."

I take a slow sip of my coffee, buying myself a moment. Nora's always been perceptive, and there's no point in sugar-coating things with her. "He's doing well, considering. But I think it's going to take him longer to heal than any of them want to admit. He's lost a lot of endurance."

"What do you mean?" Atlee asks, leaning forward with concern.

"Last night, Jesse had to help him shower, and it took them over an hour. Truett was exhausted afterward, could barely keep his eyes open." I set my mug down, running my thumb along the rim. "He's frustrated, you know? Being dependent on everyone else is killing him almost as much as the actual injury was."

Nora doesn't say anything, but I can see the worry etched in the lines around her eyes, the way she's gripping her coffee mug a little too tightly. Her knuckles are white against the ceramic.

"Nora," I say gently. "Can I ask you something?"

She nods, though I can tell she's bracing herself.

"Do you love him?"

The question hangs in the air between us like smoke. Atlee glances between us, suddenly very interested in her coffee. Nora's face goes through a series of expressions—surprise, vulnerability, and then something that looks like resignation.

"I do," she says finally, her voice barely above a whisper. "But it's complicated."

"It always is," I reply, reaching over to squeeze her hand. Her fingers are cold despite the warm mug she'd been holding. "Love isn't supposed to be easy, Nora. If it were, everyone would be doing it right."

She lets out a shaky laugh. "I keep telling myself that I should walk away. That getting involved with someone like Truett, someone who lives dangerously, who could get hurt or worse, is stupid. But then I see him lying in that bed, and all I want to do is crawl in there with him and hold him until he's better."

"Then why don't you?" Atlee asks softly. "Life's too short to waste time on what-ifs."

Nora looks at her, then at me. "Because what if I lose him? What if this shooting is just the beginning? What if next time..." She trails off, unable to finish the thought.

"What if you don't?" I counter. "What if you miss out on

something amazing because you're too scared to take the risk? Look at me and Jesse. Six months ago, if someone had told me I'd be living on a ranch in the middle of nowhere, in love with a cowboy, I would have laughed them out of the room. Especially since that particular cowboy let me down easy when I kissed him on my eighteenth birthday. But here I am, and I've never been happier."

"Even with everything that's happened?" Nora asks. "Even with the danger?"

I consider this. The shooting shook me more than I care to admit. Seeing Truett lying there, seeing Jesse's face when he thought we might lose my brother, it was terrifying. But it also showed me how precious what we have really is.

"Especially because of everything that's happened," I say. "It made me realize that none of us are guaranteed tomorrow. We might as well make today count. Am I okay knowing what they do? I'm still coming to terms with it, and they've promised me that things will change. Are they telling the truth? I guess we'll see."

Atlee nods enthusiastically. "That's exactly what I told myself when I decided to help get that medicine, even though my instincts told me not to."

"And look how that's working out for you," I tease, gesturing toward her. "Devlin's got you under his protection whether you like it or not."

She blushes again, and I can't help but grin. "He does seem to have appointed himself my personal bodyguard, doesn't he?"

"Honey, that man has been watching you like a hawk since the moment he brought you to the ranch that night," Nora says, finally cracking a smile. "The protection thing is just his excuse to keep you close."

"You think so?" Atlee's voice is hopeful, and it's adorable how transparent she is.

"I definitely think so."

We spend the next hour talking, laughing, and slowly working through the knot of worry that's been sitting in all our chests. It feels good to be with other women, to talk about feelings and fears without having to worry about appearing weak or needy. The men in our lives are wonderful, but sometimes you need your girlfriends.

When my phone buzzes with a text from Jesse saying he's on his way back, I feel that familiar flutter in my stomach. Even after all this time, the thought of seeing him makes my heart race.

"I should get dressed," I say, standing and stretching. "Jesse and Devlin are on their way back, and he promised me a good dinner."

"Before you go," Nora says, standing as well. "Thank you... for pushing me to think about what I really want instead of what I'm afraid of."

"That's what friends are for," I reply, hugging her tightly. "And Nora? Truett's tougher than he looks. He's going to be fine."

She nods, though I can tell she's still worried. We all are.

"He was with me."

The words come out steady and clear, even though my heart is pounding against my ribs. I meet Noah's gaze, grateful for the dim lighting that hopefully hides the flush I can feel creeping up my neck.

Noah has kind eyes, but there's steel underneath his gentle demeanor. He's been asking questions of the community for days, going over the night of the shooting again and again, looking for inconsistencies in our stories.

"From what time to what time?" he asks, making notes in his small notebook.

"From around seven in the evening until the next morning," I reply. "We had dinner, watched a movie, and then..." I let the implication hang in the air, hoping the blush on my cheeks sells the story.

Noah glances at me, his expression unreadable. "Aubree, do you know what's going to happen if we find out you're lying for them?"

The question sends a chill down my spine, but I force myself to maintain eye contact. "I do know, but I'm not lying, so the investigators have no leg to stand on."

It's not entirely a lie. Jesse was with me for most of that evening.

"You're sure about this?" Noah presses. "Because if Jesse was involved in what happened to those cattle—"

"He wasn't," I interrupt, perhaps a bit too forcefully. "Jesse would never do something like that."

Noah closes his notebook and studies me for a long moment. "All right," he says finally. "I think that's all I need for now. But Aubree, if you remember anything else, anything at all..."

"I'll call you," I promise, standing from the table on legs that feel slightly unsteady.

As he makes his way toward the exit, the group of us at our

table is quiet. Jesse's eyes find mine immediately, and I can see the tension in his shoulders, the worry lines around his green eyes. When I reach them, he wraps his arm around my waist, pulling me close against his side.

"You did good," he murmurs against my ear, his breath warm and comforting.

"Thank you," I whisper back.

Devlin nods toward the door. "Let's get out of here."

The four of us walk out into the evening air, and I take a deep breath, feeling like I can finally breathe properly again.

"So," Jesse says as we reach his truck, his hand still resting on the small of my back. "Does this mean you aren't going back to Chicago?"

The question catches me off guard, even though I've been expecting it.

I turn to face him, taking in his rugged features, the dark beard that frames his full mouth, those striking green eyes that seem to see straight through to my soul. This man has turned my entire world upside down, and somehow that feels exactly right.

"I'm staying," I say, loud enough for Devlin and Atlee to hear as well. "You better get used to me being here."

The smile that spreads across Jesse's face is worth every uncertainty, every fear I've had about this decision. Before I can say anything else, he picks me up and twirls me around in the parking lot, my feet leaving the ground as I laugh and wrap my arms around his neck.

"Jesse!" I squeal, half protesting, half delighted. "Put me down!"

"Not a chance," he says, spinning me once more before setting me back on my feet. His hands frame my face, thumbs brushing across my cheekbones. "You're sure? Because once you commit to this life, to me, there's no going back. You were coddled as a teenager. It won't be like that this time. Ranch life isn't easy, Aubree. Neither am I."

I reach up and trace the line of his jaw, feeling the rough texture of his beard under my fingertips. "I don't want easy," I tell him. "I want you. I want this. All of it."

He kisses me then, right there in the parking lot, with Devlin and Atlee watching. It's not a gentle kiss. It's claiming, possessive, full of promise and heat. When we finally break apart, I'm breathless and dizzy and completely, utterly in love.

"Well," Atlee says from somewhere behind us. "I guess that settles that."

I glance over to see her smiling at us, while Devlin is trying very hard to look anywhere but at us. His cheeks are actually pink, which is endearing on such a tough, silent man.

"Come on," Jesse says, opening the truck door for me. "Let's go home. Atlee, Devlin will drive you back into town."

Home. The word settles in my chest like a warm ember. This place hasn't felt like home since my parents died, but right now? I can't imagine it feeling any other way.

As Jesse drives through the darkening countryside, his hand resting on my thigh, I watch the familiar landscape roll by. This is my world now, these people are my family, and despite all the chaos and danger and uncertainty, I can't imagine being anywhere else.

I place my hand over Jesse's, where it rests on my leg, threading our fingers together.

"I love you," I say quietly, the words carrying all the weight of my decision, my commitment, my future.

"I love you too," he replies, bringing our joined hands to his lips to press a soft kiss to my knuckles. "Welcome home, Aubree."

As we turn down the long drive toward the ranch, toward our life together, I know with absolute certainty that I'm exactly where I belong.

TWENTY-FIVE
JESSE

YOU CAN'T WIPE the smile off my face, not after I've confirmed that Aubree is staying. The past few days have been filled with happiness like I've never had before. We still have to discuss where she's going to live and sleep, but that's a conversation for another day. We'll worry about that when the time comes.

"So she's staying?" Truett asks as I sit in his room, eating lunch with him.

"She is." I smile.

"I know she's staying because of you," Truett says as he struggles to sit up. "Can't say I'm surprised or disappointed, I just want her to be here."

"I do too, but if she's going to be here, we've got to make it a point to put a stop to almost everything illegal going on over here. There are still things she doesn't know about." I think of what Devlin and Carson have their hands in, but that's not my secret to tell. "She'll only know about it if she has to."

He nods, agreeing with me. "You better make her happy, Jesse. That's your one goal in life now."

"I know it is. I just want to make sure you're okay with this."

Truett's expression grows serious, and he studies my face for a long moment. The afternoon light streaming through his window catches the worry lines that have deepened since his accident, making him look older than his years. He shifts against his pillows, wincing slightly at the movement.

"Jesse," he starts, his voice carrying a weight I haven't heard before. "I've been thinking about this a lot. About you and Aubree."

My stomach tightens. "And?"

"It's not easy, you know? Watching my little sister fall in love." He runs a hand through his hair, a gesture so similar to Aubree's that it makes my chest ache. "She's always been independent, always thought she could handle everything on her own. Seeing her open up to someone, seeing her vulnerable...it scares the hell out of me."

I lean forward in my chair, setting my plate aside. "Truett..."

He holds up a hand to stop me. "Let me finish. It scares me because I know what love can do to a person. I've seen how it can build you up and tear you down. I don't want Aubree to go through that kind of pain again."

The words hit me like a punch to the gut. "I would never hurt her. You have to know that."

"I do know that," he says quietly. "That's what I'm trying to tell you. If it had to be anyone, Jesse, I'm glad it's you. You've been my best friend since we were kids. You've stuck by this family through everything. You've proven your loyalty over and over again."

Relief floods through me, but I can see there's more he wants to say.

"You know her better than most people do," he continues. "You've seen her at her worst and her best. You know how stubborn she can be, how fierce she is when she loves someone. You know what she's been through.

"She deserves someone who sees all of that and loves her anyway. Someone who won't try to change her or dim her light. Someone who'll stand beside her, not in front of her or behind her, but right there with her through whatever comes next."

"That's all I want to do," I tell him honestly. "I want to be her partner in everything."

Truett's eyes meet mine, and I see a mixture of trust and warning there. "She's going to fight you sometimes. She's going to try to handle things on her own because that's what she's always done. She's going to push you away when things get tough because she's afraid of being a burden."

"I know."

"And you're going to have to be patient with her. You're going to have to prove over and over again that you're not going anywhere, that you're in this for the long haul."

"I am," I say firmly. "I'm not going anywhere, Truett. Not ever."

He studies my face for another long moment, then nods slowly. "I trust you, Jesse. I trust you with the most important thing in my life. That's not something I say lightly."

The weight of his words settles over me like a mantle. "Thank you. I know what she means to you, and I promise you, I'll spend every day making sure she knows what she means to me."

"I've been taking care of her for most of her life, but she needs something different now," Truett says softly. "It's time she feels that love from someone else. She needs someone to take care of her. Really take care of her, not just the surface stuff. The deep stuff. The parts of herself she keeps hidden because she thinks they're too much or not enough."

I think about the way Aubree smiled this morning when she thought no one was looking, the way she hummed softly while making coffee, how she'd unconsciously reached for my hand when we were sitting on the porch last night. Those small, unguarded moments that showed me glimpses of who she was when she wasn't trying to be strong for everyone else.

"I see those parts of her," I tell him. "And I love every single one."

Truett's smile is genuine now, reaching his eyes for the first time in this conversation. "I know you do. That's why I can let go of the worry, at least about this. About you two."

"What do you mean?"

"I mean, I can stop feeling like I need to protect her from getting her heart broken by the wrong guy, because you're not the wrong guy. You're exactly who she needs, even if it took you way too long to figure it out."

I laugh, some of the tension leaving my shoulders. "I'm pretty blind, aren't I?"

"Blind as a bat," he agrees. "I knew she threw herself at you before, and I knew you let her down easy."

"Why didn't you ever say anything?"

Truett shrugs. "Because it had to be real. If I'd pushed, it might have happened sooner, but it wouldn't have been right.

You both had to come to it on your own terms, in your own time. Love can't be forced."

"No," I agree, thinking of how natural it felt when Aubree finally kissed me, how right it was when we finally stopped fighting what was between us. "It can't."

"Besides," Truett adds with a grin that reminds me of the boy I grew up with. "Now I get to watch you deal with all her quirks and habits. Do you know she rearranges furniture when she's stressed?"

I laugh. "I do now."

"And she hates when people leave dishes in the sink overnight."

"Noted."

"Oh, and she's absolutely terrible at directions. Gets lost going to places she's been a hundred times."

"I'll make sure to drive."

Truett's laughter turns into a cough, and I can see the exhaustion creeping into his features. The conversation has taken a lot out of him, but I can tell he needed to say these things.

"I should let you rest," I say, standing from my chair.

"Yeah," he agrees, settling back against his pillows. "But Jesse?"

"Yeah?"

"Thank you."

"For what?"

"For loving her the way she deserves to be loved. For seeing her the way she deserves to be seen. For being the man she deserves."

The gratitude in his voice nearly undoes me. "Thank you for trusting me with her."

"Take care of her, Jesse. And let her take care of you too. She needs to feel needed, but not in the way that everyone depends on her for everything. Take care of her with love and respect. Like you want her to be part of your life, not because you need her to fix things or solve problems, but because you can't imagine your life without her in it."

"I can't," I tell him honestly. "I tried for years to imagine it, and I can't."

"Good," Truett says, his eyes already drifting closed. "Then you're exactly where you're supposed to be."

I leave him to rest, my mind turning over everything he's said. The weight of his trust, his blessing, settles into my bones like an oath. I won't let him down. More importantly, I won't let Aubree down.

The afternoon sun is warm on my face as I walk toward the barn, my heart lighter than it's been in years. I can hear movement inside, the sound of a pitchfork scraping against concrete, and I know without looking that Aubree is in there working.

I find her in the third stall, mucking it out with more force than necessary. Her honey-blonde hair is pulled back in a messy ponytail, loose strands curling around her face in the humid air. She's wearing an old tank top and jeans that hug her curves in all the right ways, and there's a light sheen of sweat on her skin that makes my mouth go dry.

She doesn't hear me approach, too focused on her task, muttering under her breath about stubborn horses and lazy ranch hands. I lean against the stall door, content to watch her for a moment. There's something about seeing her like this, sleeves rolled up and working hard, that makes my chest tight with affection.

"You know," I say finally. "I'm sure you could pay high school kids to do that for you."

She jumps, spinning around with the pitchfork still in her hands. When she sees me, her startled expression melts into a smile that makes my knees weak.

"You scared me," she accuses, but there's no real anger in it.

"Sorry," I say, pushing off from the door frame and stepping into the stall with her. "I was just enjoying the view."

She rolls her eyes, but I can see the flush creeping up her neck. "The view of me shoveling horse manure? Your standards have really dropped, Jesse."

"My standards are exactly where they should be," I tell her, moving closer. "High enough to appreciate a beautiful woman who's not afraid to get her hands dirty."

She opens her mouth to respond, but I'm close enough now to see the way her breath catches, the way her pupils dilate slightly. The pitchfork is still between us, but I reach around it to cup her face with one hand.

"Besides," I murmur, my thumb brushing across her cheek, "I like seeing you here. In the barn, on the ranch. It feels right."

"Jesse," she whispers, and I love the way my name sounds on her lips.

I take the pitchfork from her hands, setting it aside before backing her gently against the wall. My hands find her waist, fingers spanning across the soft curves there, and I feel her hands come up to rest against my chest.

"I talked to Truett," I tell her, my voice low.

"What did he say?" There's a note of worry in her voice, and

I hate that she's still not sure of her place here, still not confident in what we have.

"He gave us his blessing," I say, watching relief flood her features. "He said if you had to fall in love with someone, he's glad it's me."

Her laugh is soft and a little watery. "He said that?"

"He did. Among other things." I lean down, pressing my forehead against hers. "He also said I better take good care of you."

"And what did you tell him?"

"I told him that was already my top priority."

She smiles up at me, and I can see something shift in her expression, some last wall crumbling away. "I love you, Jesse."

The words hit me like lightning, even though she's said them before. I don't think I'll ever get tired of hearing them.

"I love you too," I tell her, and then I'm kissing her, tasting the salt of her skin and the sweetness that's purely her.

Her hands fist in my shirt, pulling me closer, and I press her back against the wooden wall. The barn around us fades away until there's nothing but the feel of her lips against mine, the way she melts into my touch, the soft sounds she makes that drive me absolutely crazy.

When we finally break apart, we're both breathing hard. Her lips are swollen from my kisses, her cheeks flushed, and I have to fight the urge to carry her out of this barn and straight to my bed.

"We should probably finish the stalls," she says, but her voice is husky, and her hands are still gripping my shirt.

"Probably," I agree, but I make no move to step away from her.

She laughs, the sound echoing in the space between us. "You're not making this easy."

"I'm not trying to," I admit. "I like having you close."

"I like being close," she says, and the honesty in her voice makes my chest tighten.

I force myself to step back, to give us both some breathing room. But I catch her hand in mine, linking our fingers together.

"Are you happy, Aubree?" I ask her, suddenly needing to know. "Really happy?"

She looks up at me, her deep brown eyes soft and warm. "Happier than I've ever been," she says without hesitation. "I spent so many years thinking I knew what I wanted, thinking I had to leave here to find it. But everything I was looking for was right here all along."

"Even me?" I tease, but there's a serious note underneath it.

"Especially you," she says, squeezing my hand. "I knew it back then, but you made me work for it."

I laugh. "I made you work for it? You're the one who left."

"Because I was embarrassed and terrified," she admits. "I was terrified of ruining the friendship we had—that you had with Truett—if I convinced you to give us a chance and then things went wrong."

"You're not going to lose me," I tell her firmly. "Not ever. You're stuck with me now."

"Good," she says, rising up on her toes to press a quick kiss to my lips. "Because I'm not letting you go either."

We stand there for a moment, just looking at each other, and I marvel at how different everything feels now. How the air between us has changed, charged with possibility and promise.

"What about you?" she asks suddenly. "Are you happy?"

I consider the question, thinking about everything that's led us to this moment. The years of friendship, the careful distance we maintained, the fear and uncertainty, and finally, finally, the moment when we stopped fighting what was between us.

"Yes," I tell her, and the certainty in my voice surprises even me. "All because a beautiful woman tempted me with a kiss."

Her smile is radiant, lighting up her entire face. "Just one kiss?"

"Well," I say, pulling her closer again. "Maybe it was more than one."

"Maybe it was," she agrees, and then she's kissing me again, soft and sweet and full of promise.

When we break apart this time, I rest my chin on top of her head, breathing in the scent of her hair, the smell of sunshine and hay that clings to her skin.

"We should really finish these stalls," she says again, but she makes no move to pull away from me.

"We should," I agree. "But first, there's something I want to ask you."

She pulls back to look at me, curiosity in her eyes. "What?"

"Move in with me," I say, the words tumbling out before I can second-guess them. "I know we said we'd figure out the logistics later, but I don't want to wait. I want to wake up next to you every morning. I want to fall asleep with you in my arms every night. I want to build a life with you, starting now. I'll even build you a fireplace like the one here."

Her eyes widen, and for a moment I think maybe I've moved too fast, pushed too hard. But then her face breaks into a smile that could power the entire ranch.

"Yes," she says, laughing. "Yes, of course, yes."

And as I spin her around in the middle of that barn, her laughter echoing off the rafters, I think about how perfect this moment is. How right it feels to have her here, in my arms, choosing me the same way I choose her.

When I set her down, she's still smiling, still glowing with happiness. "I can't believe this is real," she says.

"It's real," I assure her. "We're real."

She nods, and I can see her trying to process everything, trying to wrap her mind around the fact that she's finally home, finally where she belongs.

"Now," I say, picking up the pitchfork and handing it back to her. "Let's finish these stalls so we can go celebrate properly."

She takes the pitchfork, but she's still smiling that radiant smile. "What kind of celebration did you have in mind?"

"The kind that involves a lot less clothing and a lot more privacy," I tell her, and her cheeks flush pink.

"Jesse!" she protests, but she's laughing.

"What? I'm just saying, we have a lot of time to make up for."

She shakes her head, but she's still smiling as she gets back to work. And as I watch her, as I help her finish the last few stalls, I can't help but think about how different my life was just a few days ago. How empty it seems now in comparison.

The sun is starting to set by the time we're done, painting the sky in shades of orange and pink that match the warmth spreading through my chest. Aubree is tired, her hair even messier now, dirt on her jeans, and contentment in her eyes.

"Ready to go home?" I ask her, taking her hand.

She looks up at me, and the way she smiles makes my heart skip a beat.

"With you?" she says. "I'm ready for anything."

And as we walk out of that barn together, hands linked, faces turned toward the sunset, I know that whatever comes next, we'll face it together. We'll build something beautiful here, something lasting. We'll create the kind of love story that Truett talked about, the kind that withstands anything life throws at it.

Because she's right. We're ready for anything, as long as we're together.

TWENTY-SIX
ATLEE

IT'S BEEN the slowest day here at the pharmacy, probably because it's so hot outside. Summer has hit in full force here in Grizzly River, and most everyone is tubing on the town's namesake. I wish like fuck I were there right now, but someone has to man the pharmacy, and since I'm the low man on the totem pole, that's me.

"You sure you're going to be okay here by yourself?"

Exasperation makes me answer with an exaggerated, "Yes, just because I'm stuck here doesn't mean you should be too, Pay." My coworker, Payton, has been nice enough to stay with me, but now that we have an hour until closing, it doesn't seem like there's any sense in her staying.

"All right, but if you need anything, you can call me."

"I know. I'm sure I'll be fine."

I watch as she clocks out and leaves, wishing like hell that I could go with her. These last sixty minutes are going to be the longest of my life. Grabbing my phone, I start scrolling through social media, stopping on the pictures that Aubree has posted of the Nelson brothers.

Devlin. The strong, silent type. He's so fucking hot. Older than I should be attracted to. A whole decade separates us, but I can't stop thinking about him. Not since he came to get me the night that Truett was shot. He and I text sometimes, and talk sometimes too, but it's never gone any further than that.

I'm glancing down at a picture of him when the bell rings, signaling a customer. I glance up and greet them with a smile, but my blood runs cold, and the smile is quickly wiped off my face.

The man standing in front of me is wearing a black ski mask despite the sweltering heat, and there's something metallic glinting in his right hand. My heart stops beating for a full second before it kicks back into overdrive, hammering against my ribs so hard I'm sure he can hear it.

"Don't make a fucking sound," he growls, his voice muffled but menacing. He steps closer to the counter, and I can see his eyes through the holes in the mask—cold, desperate, wild. The gun in his hand shakes slightly, but not enough to give me any comfort. "I want everything you've got in the narcotics safe. Now."

My mouth goes dry as sandpaper. "I-I can't get into the safe," I stammer, my voice barely above a whisper. "I don't have the combination. Only my boss can—"

"Bullshit!" He slams his free hand on the counter, making me jump back. "You work here. You can get into it. Don't lie to me!"

"I'm not lying," I insist, my hands trembling as I hold them up in surrender. "I swear to God, I'm just a pharmacy tech. The pharmacist has to be here to access the controlled substances. It's the law."

His eyes narrow, and I can see him weighing whether to believe me. The seconds stretch out like hours, my pulse thundering in my ears.

"Fine," he finally spits. "Call your boss. Tell them to get down here and open it. And if you try anything stupid, I'll put a bullet in you before you can blink."

I nod frantically, reaching for the phone with shaking hands. But instead of calling my boss, my fingers automatically dial the number I've memorized by heart. Devlin's number.

Please pick up, please pick up, please...

"Atlee?" His deep voice comes through the speaker, and relief floods through me so intensely, I nearly collapse.

"Hi, Mr. Patterson," I say, trying to keep my voice steady while the masked man leans closer to listen. "I need you to come down to the pharmacy right away. There's been a...situation that requires your immediate attention."

There's a pause, and I can practically hear Devlin's mind working. He knows I don't call him Mr. Patterson. Ever.

"Atlee, what's wrong?" His voice is sharp now, alert.

"Yes, sir, I understand this is unusual, but I need you to access the narcotics safe. There's someone here who needs..." I glance at the gunman. "Who needs you to open it immediately."

"Jesus Christ," Devlin breathes. "Are you in danger? Is someone there with a weapon?"

"Yes, that's correct. How soon can you be here?"

"I'm five minutes out. I was heading to town anyway. Stay calm, sweetheart. I'm coming."

The endearment makes my eyes well up with tears, but I blink them back. "Thank you, sir. I'll see you soon."

I hang up and look at the masked man. "He's on his way. Five minutes."

But something in his posture has changed. He's studying me with those cold eyes, and I realize with growing horror that he's figured it out.

"That wasn't your boss, was it?" he says slowly, his voice deadly quiet.

"Of course it was."

"Bullshit!" He vaults over the counter before I can react, grabbing me by the arm and yanking me against him. The barrel of the gun presses against my temple, cold and unforgiving. "You called someone else. Who was it? Your boyfriend? The cops?"

"No, I swear. It was my boss."

He backhands me across the face with his free hand, and pain explodes through my cheek. I cry out, tasting blood where my teeth cut the inside of my mouth.

"Don't fucking lie to me!" He shakes me hard enough to rattle my teeth. "I heard how you talked to him. Nobody talks to their boss like that."

Tears stream down my face as he presses the gun harder against my head. "Please, I didn't call the police. I promise I didn't call the police."

"Then who?" He grabs a fistful of my hair and yanks my head back. "Who did you call?"

"A friend," I whisper. "Just a friend. He's not a cop, I swear."

"Well, your friend better stay the hell away, or I'll blow your pretty little brains all over this pharmacy." He drags me toward the back of the store, away from the windows. "And then I'll hunt him down and kill him too."

My knees nearly give out at the threat. Not Devlin. I can't let anything happen to Devlin because of my stupidity.

"Please," I beg. "Just take what you want and leave. He won't interfere, I promise."

"Shut up." He's pacing now, agitated, the gun never leaving my head. "Shut the fuck up and let me think."

The next few minutes are the longest of my life. Every second feels like an eternity as I wait for either Devlin to arrive or for this maniac to decide he's done with me. My face throbs where he hit me, and I can feel my cheek swelling.

Then I hear it, the soft chime of the front door.

"Atlee?" Devlin's voice carries through the store, carefully controlled but with an undercurrent of barely contained fury.

The gunman tightens his grip on me. "Don't say a word," he hisses in my ear.

"I'm back here," I call out, unable to stop myself. I need Devlin to know where we are, even if it puts him in danger.

The masked man curses and presses the gun harder against my skull. "You stupid bitch."

Heavy footsteps approach, and then Devlin appears at the end of the aisle. When he sees us, me with a gun to my head, my face already showing the beginnings of a bruise, his entire body goes rigid. His hands clench into fists at his sides, and his dark eyes fill with a rage so intense it makes me shiver.

"Let her go," he says, his voice deadly calm. "Whatever you want, we can work it out. Just let her go."

"Back off, cowboy," the gunman snarls. "One more step and she's dead."

"You hurt her again, and you'll be the one who's dead," Devlin replies with such quiet certainty that even the masked man seems to falter for a second.

"I want the drugs," the man says, his voice cracking slightly. "Just give me the fucking drugs and I'll leave."

"Fine. But you let her go first."

"Hell no. She's my insurance."

They stare each other down, and I can feel the tension crackling between them like electricity before a storm. I need to do something—anything—to help. My eyes dart around desperately and land on the panic button under the counter, just a few feet away.

If I can just reach it...

"Look," Devlin says, taking a small step forward. "I can see you're desperate. Maybe you need the pills for someone you care about. I get that. But hurting an innocent woman isn't going to solve your problems."

"Don't pretend you understand shit about my problems!" the man screams, and in his agitation, his grip on me loosens just slightly.

It's the chance I need. I throw my elbow back into his ribs as hard as I can and break free from his grasp, diving for the panic button. I slam my palm down on it just as the gun goes off.

The sound is deafening in the small space, and I scream, certain I've been shot. But then Devlin is there, tackling the gunman to the ground. They roll across the floor, fighting for control of the weapon.

"Atlee, get out of here!" Devlin grunts as he struggles with the masked man.

But I can't move. I'm frozen in terror, watching the two men fight for what I know is my life. The gun clatters across the linoleum, and both men lunge for it.

The gunman gets there first, but Devlin grabs his wrist, forcing the weapon away from us. They're both strong, but Devlin has years of ranch work behind him, and slowly, inexorably, he begins to overpower the smaller man.

"You son of a bitch," Devlin snarls, slamming the gunman's hand against the floor until he's forced to release the weapon. "You put your hands on her."

He pins the man to the ground with his knee and draws back his fist. The punch connects with a sickening crack that I feel in my bones.

"Devlin, stop!" I cry out as he draws back for another blow. "You'll kill him!"

But before he can throw another punch, the front door bursts open and Noah Sanchez rushes in, his service weapon drawn.

"Sheriff's department!" he shouts. "Everyone on the ground!"

"It's okay, Noah," I call out shakily. "Devlin's got him."

Noah quickly assesses the situation and holsters his weapon, pulling out his handcuffs instead. "Step back, Devlin. I've got this."

Devlin reluctantly moves aside, allowing Noah to cuff the gunman, who's groaning and barely conscious on the floor. His mask has come off during the struggle, revealing a gaunt face I don't recognize, probably someone from outside Grizzly River, desperate enough to try robbing a small-town pharmacy.

"You okay, Atlee?" Noah asks as he hauls the man to his feet.

I nod, though I'm anything but okay. My whole body is shaking, and the adrenaline is making me feel sick and lightheaded.

"I need to get this piece of shit to the station," Noah says. "I'll need statements from both of you, but that can wait until tomorrow. You've been through enough this afternoon."

As Noah leads the gunman away, I finally allow myself to look at Devlin. Really look at him. His shirt is torn, there's a cut above his left eyebrow, and his knuckles are bloody. But his eyes...God, his eyes are full of something I've never seen there before.

"Atlee," he breathes, and then I'm in his arms.

He holds me so tight I can barely breathe, but I don't care. I bury my face in his chest and let the tears come. All the fear, the terror, the helplessness, it all pours out of me in great, heaving sobs.

"Shhh," he murmurs into my hair. "You're safe now. I've got you."

"He was going to kill me," I choke out. "If you hadn't come."

"But I did come," he says fiercely, pulling back to cup my face in his hands. His thumb gently traces the bruise on my cheek, and his jaw tightens with fresh anger. "And I always will. Do you hear me, Atlee? I will always come for you."

The intensity in his voice, in his eyes, takes my breath away. This isn't just about tonight. This is about something much bigger, much deeper.

"Devlin," I whisper.

He closes his eyes, his jaw working. "I've never been so terrified in my life."

My heart stops, then starts again at double speed. "You were worried about me?"

He opens his eyes and looks at me with such raw honesty, it makes my chest tight. "I was scared shitless. Afraid I was going to lose you. I care too fuckin' much, even though I know I shouldn't be. You're ten years younger than me. You deserve someone who—"

I cut him off by pressing my lips to his. The kiss is desperate, full of all the fear and relief and longing that's been building between us for months. He tastes like coffee and something distinctly him, and I never want to stop kissing him.

When we finally break apart, we're both breathing hard.

"I don't care about the age difference," I tell him. "I don't care about anything except how I feel when I'm with you. How safe you make me feel. How right this feels."

"Atlee." My name is a prayer on his lips.

"I was so scared he was going to hurt you," I admit. "When I heard you come in, all I could think was that I'd put you in danger too, and I couldn't bear it."

"Hey." He tilts my chin up, forcing me to meet his eyes. "Listen to me. Nothing, and I mean nothing, was going to stop me from getting to you today. And nothing ever will. You understand me?"

I nod, tears spilling over again.

"I promise you," he says, his voice thick with emotion. "I am never going to let anything happen to you again. You're mine now, Atlee. Mine to protect, mine to care for. And I don't give a damn who has a problem with it."

The possessiveness in his voice should probably scare me, but instead, it makes me feel cherished. Protected. Loved.

"Yours," I agree, and the word feels like coming home.

He kisses me again, gentler this time but no less passionate. And as he holds me in the aftermath of the worst night of my life, I finally understand what it means to feel completely, utterly safe.

Devlin Nelson is going to be the death of me, but he just might be my salvation too. And I'm ready for whatever comes next, as long as he's by my side.

A LOOK AT BOOK TWO

BRANDED

Some hearts are worth stealing... even if the consequences are deadly.

When Atlee Walsh is attacked at the pharmacy where she works, the last person she expects to save her is Devlin Nelson. The oldest of the infamous Nelson brothers. A rugged and distant ex-soldier. A man with a reputation as dark as the past he won't talk about.

After Devlin spirits her away to his remote cabin to recover, Atlee knows she should be scared. But all she feels is safe. Wanted. She can't ignore the simmering attraction between them. And when the walls between them break, the quiet strength behind his silence becomes impossible to resist.

But danger isn't far behind. With a corrupt deputy obsessed with bringing the Nelson brothers down, and powerful enemies closing in, Atlee uncovers a truth she isn't ready for: the cattle rustling that's kept the ranch afloat... and the man she's falling for at the center of it.

In a small town where water rights determine survival and old grudges never die, Atlee and Devlin will have to fight not just for their love, but for their lives. Because some men will do anything to get revenge, even use the woman Devlin loves against him.

AVAILABLE MARCH 2026

Laramie Briscoe is the *USA Today* and *Wall Street Journal* bestselling author of over thirty books, with sales of over half a million copies.

Since self-publishing her first book in May of 2013, Laramie has appeared on the Top 100 Bestselling E-books Lists on Amazon Kindle, Apple Books, Barnes & Noble, and Kobo. Her books have been known to make readers laugh and cry. They are guaranteed to be emotional, steamy reads.

When she's not writing alpha males who seriously love their women, she loves spending time with friends, reading, and marathoning shows on Netflix. Married to her high school sweetheart, Laramie lives in Bowling Green, Kentucky, with her husband (the Travel Coordinator) and an adorable dog named Gus.

www.laramiebriscoe.net

www.ingramcontent.com/pod-product-compliance
Lightning Source LLC
LaVergne TN
LVHW041250110826
845146LV00005BA/1330

9798895677216